We Won't Go Back

Books by Charlene Wexler

Farewell To South Shore Series
Book 1: Farewell to South Shore
Book 2: We Won't Go Back

Laughter And Tears Series
Book 1: Lori
Book 2: Murder Across the Ocean

NOVELS
Murder on Skid Row

COMING SOON!

Laughter And Tears Series
Book 3: Milk and Oranges
Book 4: Elephants in the Room

**For more information
visit:** SpeakingVolumes.us

We Won't Go Back

Charlene Wexler

SPEAKING VOLUMES, LLC
NAPLES, FLORIDA
2025

We Won't Go Back

Copyright © 2025 by Charlene Wexler

All rights reserved. No part of this book may be reproduced or transmitted in any form or by any means without written permission.

ISBN 979-8-89022-317-3

This book is dedicated to my three granddaughters,
Lily, Bella, and Sage. Their generation must make sure that
WE WON'T GO BACK

Acknowledgments

Thank you to my publishers, Erica and Kurt Mueller; my editor, William S. Bike; my agent, Nancy Rosenfeld; and my family and friends who helped bring We Won't Go Back to everyone.

Chapter One

Babs froze as she watched the breaking news on television. In that moment, the world seemed to turn upside down as she contemplated the horrible consequences of such a shocking headline.

UNITED STATES SUPREME COURT CONSIDERS REVERSING ROE V. WADE.

Her two daughters barely noticed as they leaned against their sofa pillows, immersed in their phones. Stacy, 13, didn't even look up as Lori, 17, asked her mother what was going on. Babs was too shocked to reply.

"Mom, what is Roe v. Wade?"

"Yeah, why are you so upset?"

"Really, girls? Are you serious?"

They both dove straight back into their phones.

Babs nervously twirled a lock of hair around her fingers.

How could my daughters not know what this is? Lori's old enough to get pregnant, God forbid, but how could she not know? My mother and her friends worked so hard to make abortion legal. Did I never mention that to the girls? This is all my fault for not keeping them informed about their grandmother and women's rights.

Babs gathered herself and tried not to shout.

"Roe v. Wade refers to a Supreme Court decision made in 1973 that gave women the constitutional right to have an abortion."

Oh, my God. That damn conservative court wouldn't dare. It's 50 years since it became law. How could this happen now? Women are

CEOs. They run companies. They're Senators, Representatives, and even a Vice President!

Babs shook her head and bit her lip as she flipped to another station and checked her phone for a text or Facebook message to verify what she had just seen. Suddenly, her phone buzzed with texts, and reporters on the scene in Washington confirmed the rumor. The young anchorwoman looked confused, as if she wasn't aware of Roe. v Wade, either.

When things are good, we quit paying attention. That needs to end right now.

Babs felt her blood boil. She turned to her girls and shook their pillows.

"Mom, what are you doing?"

"Just listen now. This news is horrible. It's so horrible that it's the first time in thirty years that I am glad my mother, God bless her soul, isn't around to hear it."

"Mom, you are acting weird."

Stacy picked up her backpack and as she headed toward the door Babs grabbed her arm.

"Don't leave, please. Not now. This is an emergency. We need to go see my mother's friend, Shirley, a retired lawyer whose career was devoted to women's causes. She just messaged me about a quick meeting with a collection of women who are deeply concerned about this news. It's our duty to go."

"What? Mom, it's Saturday. My friends are waiting for me at the mall. Joanie's mother is on the way to pick me up."

Stacy, a petite, thin pixie with enormous green eyes, stood and stared at her mother. She typically whined and maneuvered her way in and out of things she did or didn't want to do, and going to a meeting of boisterous, disgruntled older women was not high on her list of something fun to do on a weekend.

Lori, a tall thin beauty, was the shy and obedient one, but she wasn't terribly enthusiastic about driving into Chicago either.

Babs turned off the television, grabbed her purse, threw a jacket at her youngest, and gave her oldest a friendly shove off the sofa toward the door.

"Both of you are coming with me. No arguments. I told you. This is an emergency, and it affects *all* women. And girls, too! Invite your friends to join us. We must do something!"

As Babs texted Shirley that she was coming, Stacy stamped her feet and made sure that her mother could see her tighten her upper lip in an angry expression. She texted her friend and followed her sister outside to her mom's new silver Lexus. Lori noticed that her defiant little sister had left her jacket on the sofa.

Bad move, girl.

A 40-degree wind hit them all in the face. Babs stared at her youngest daughter, who was already sulking in the backseat.

She is just like my brother, always on the attack. I wish I knew where Jim was right now.

Jim was like their father, a passionate supporter of the conservative movement. Back in 2020, when Babs tried to have a logical conversation with him about politics, he blew up and disappeared from her life. Now, two years later, nothing had changed.

Jim has always been difficult, but I can't believe he still won't answer any of my attempts to contact him, especially now, when we need to talk about our father. But that will have to wait. I have two young women to educate.

As they left their home in suburban Lake Forest and drove south on the expressway to downtown Chicago, Babs and Lori discussed abortion and why Roe v. Wade shouldn't be overturned, under any circumstances.

Forty minutes later, they pulled up in front of a glass-and-metal high-rise on Chicago's fashionable Oak Street, left the car to the doorman, waved at the guard who knew them, entered the marble and wood elevator, and pushed the button for Floor 21. Lori was eager to meet her mom's friends, while Stacy dragged her feet, wishing to be anywhere else.

Rachel, Shirley's wife, welcomed them into the condo. She wore a long orange and green dress with matching sandals. She looked like she could have stepped right out of a late 60s rally for the Equal Rights Amendment. She had the same burning light in her eyes that Babs associated with the feminists of that time, which included her mother.

"The phone's been ringing nonstop all morning, and the girls have been filing in. It's time to get to work."

They walked through the living room, decorated in 1970s-style, black-and-white foil-wallpaper, into a fully mirrored dining room. There sat 80-year-old Shirley, dressed in a silk, brown and white striped blouse over tan slacks. Her shiny white hair, cut to perfection, emphasized her pearl necklace and matching earrings. She had always dressed in the latest fashions, which belied her fierce commitment to women's issues. She was surrounded by a group of women she referred to as "The Girls," a codename they used among themselves as a pro-abortion group. Except for Babs, they were at least 70 years old and dressed professionally, as if they were ready to march into a courtroom and set the world straight on how things should be. Babs and her daughters were in jeans, which Stacy didn't hesitate to point out. Babs shushed her and pointed to her phone, which Stacy reluctantly put in her pocket.

Shirley got up, steadied herself with one manicured hand on her chair, and turned to Babs. With open arms, she embraced her in a warm hug, which Lori noticed.

We Won't Go Back

"Babs, I knew you would come. With your girls, too. Stacy, you must've had your Bat Mitzvah by now. How wonderful. Rachel, please get these young ladies some cookies. Like I always say, protesters need to be well fed!"

Babs sat down on the beige silk sofa facing a ceiling-to-floor picture window that overlooked Lake Michigan. From the 21st floor, the boats and the people around the clear blue lake looked like moving toys. She had only lived in houses.

What a different perspective from up here. It's almost as if we could conduct the events below, but unfortunately, the reality is quite different on the ground.

Babs patted the sofa to signal Lori and Stacy to join her.

"Shirley, my teenage daughters don't know much at all about Roe. I guess that's probably my fault. We've all taken it for granted. At least I have. Please tell them why this is such an important decision for all women and girls."

There was a collective hush in the room from the other women sitting around Shirley. She took off her glasses and wiped them clean on a silk handkerchief before talking, as if she wanted the two young girls to understand the gravity of the moment. Finally, she turned her head and directed her conversation to Lori and Stacy.

"Back in the dinosaur days when I was growing up, women were expected to follow the status quo of the time. Get married, stay home, and watch the house and children. The only jobs open to women were factory laborer, secretary, nurse, or teacher. Women couldn't get credit cards in their own name. They got fired when they got pregnant. They couldn't go to Ivy League schools or get into law school or medical school. They couldn't earn equal pay with men, take legal action against sexual harassment, get birth control counseling, or have abortions."

All the women around the table nodded as Shirley continued.

"Against all odds, your grandmother, Sherrie, and I went to law school. We were the exception, not the rule. I was the only woman in a class of eighty, and it wasn't easy competing with the men. They told us we were taking up space where a man should be because, according to them, we would just work a few years and then have kids and stay home. We tried to do both and ended up tired all the time and eventually divorced. But we opened the door for future generations, and we won't go back under any circumstances."

Stacy jumped in.

"We read about how women worked to get the vote back then. I can't believe you had to fight just to vote. That's so stupid."

Shirley stared at her and smiled.

"That was at the beginning of the twentieth century, Stacy. I'm talking about just fifty years ago, in the 1970s, just after your mother was born. That's really what it was like."

Stacy sank into her seat, seemingly overwhelmed by all the information, while Lori giggled softly and looked at Shirley, eager to hear more.

Eleanor, tanned and wrinkled and dressed in a purple knit suit, leaned forward to speak.

"Shirley, with all due respect, get to the point. We need to decide what action we are taking today. Most of us can no longer drive at night."

The doorbell rang, and two more of "The Girls" joined them at the table.

Shirley took a sip of her coffee before continuing.

"In 1973, Texas legally banned abortion. The case was called Roe versus Wade, and it made its way up to the Supreme Court. On January 22, 1973, the Supreme Court issued a seven to two decision in favor of

Roe, which stipulated that women in the U.S. have a fundamental right to choose if they wish to have an abortion. This ruling rendered the Texas abortion ban to be unconstitutional."

Stacy looked up from her phone and nodded. Lori's eyes were glued to Shirley, who pulled a tissue out of her pocket, blew her nose, and continued.

"Today, the Supreme Court is contemplating reversing that ruling and letting each state decide separately. It looks like they've telegraphed where they are going with this, and it will become a nightmare for everyone a lot sooner than we realize."

Linda, dressed perfectly in a blue pantsuit, chimed in with a happy smile on her face: "Shirley, do you remember? Did we have fun celebrating back in '73, or what? The champagne was flowing. I was at your office, and so was Sherrie. I'm talking about your grandmother, girls. Babs, your mother and I never thought our daughters would have to endure back-alley abortions again, or unwanted pregnancies, due to rape. None of that. You know how it is, whether it's due to youth, a missing father, a sexual disease, or the inability to care for a child. All these issues are part of reproductive care, and never, I mean never would we have believed back then that fifty years later we would be fighting for the same cause."

Margaret nodded.

"You said it, Linda. I was there, too. We were so happy and so young and naive."

Stacy and Lori looked at each other. Shirley nodded to them and continued.

"Besides abortion, cases of domestic abuse and harassment in the workplace are skyrocketing, too. If we don't fight, we will lose every woman's right we've gained in the last fifty years."

Rachel passed around a tray of poppyseed cookies, her trademark.

"We can't go out on our own, especially at our age. We need to coordinate with other groups. I am in touch with Karen from Illinois Planned Parenthood and with a young lawyer who hopes to get a law through Congress to make abortion legal everywhere. I will let everyone know by e-mail or message what our next move will be, probably a rally with petitions. It is so good to be active again and have your support. Thanks to all of you girls for coming."

Shirley looked around the table and then at Stacy and Lori, as if to let them know that it was also up to the next generation to carry the torch. Stacy shrugged and turned toward her mother with her puppy-dog pleading eyes.

"Mom, please don't protest again. Remember when you embarrassed me over Dr. Seuss's book being taken out of the library? The kids teased me, so can you please stay home?"

Babs rolled her eyes.

"Stacy, I think you don't understand. My mother and Shirley were diligent in protesting against anything that compromised or handicapped women's rights, whether it was abortion or equal pay or whatever. Your life would be different if not for women like them."

It was Stacy's turn to roll her eyes, but Lori stopped her. Shirley shook her head when she overheard Babs.

"You are right about me, but not your mother. Sherrie helped from behind the scenes as much as she could because she was afraid of your father even after the divorce. By the way, how is dear Ronnie? I haven't heard much about him lately. Didn't he become some bigshot in Washington during the last administration?"

Babs crossed her legs and fiddled with her shirt ties.

What can I say in front of Stacy and Lori?

She nervously twirled a lock of hair around her fingers.

"Shirley, my father and I are on opposite poles as far as politics are concerned. He was raised in a very conservative family and has always been a Republican. We barely talk."

Babs wasn't about to betray her father by exposing the truth out about his condition. It wasn't the right time, and she didn't want to add to any confusion for her daughters.

Eleanor stood up, grabbed her lion-head cane, and approached Shirley.

"Remember when extended families lived together and yelled at each other until Papa came home and told everyone to work it out?"

Shirley smiled.

"That's right. He'd say, 'You will because I said so.'"

Eleanor laughed.

"Ha! The good old days."

Shirley nodded.

"I don't think so. Believe me, girls, we won't allow it to go back to how it was before 1973, when men like Papa ruled the roost. We women won't stay in the background."

Lori took notice of Eleanor and Shirley's banter and elbowed Stacy to listen. As the other women said their goodbyes, Stacy followed them to the elevator while Lori patiently waited for Babs to hug Shirley.

As they drove home quietly, Stacy texted a friend, worried that her mom would embarrass her again, while Lori made plans to meet her boyfriend that night. Babs remembered her mother making signs and pamphlets for the many rallies they attended together.

I should set a better example for my girls.

Chapter Two

Babs stood in front of Stacy's bedroom door, took a deep breath, and knocked. She waited and knocked again. When there was still no answer, she pushed open the door, walked to the bed, and pulled the covers off Stacy, who looked so innocent in her fuzzy pink pajamas.

Babs tried to sound like a parent in control.

"Okay, what is going on here? Two days staying home from school and hiding in your bedroom doesn't work. If you're sick, we'll go to the doctor. Otherwise, you're going to school."

Stacy turned over, jumped out of bed, and pointed a finger at her mother.

"I hate you! My friends at school call you a baby killer."

Babs steadied herself before answering.

"We are *not* baby killers. None of us who support the right to have an abortion are any such thing. We are fighting for women to have the right to choose. That's it."

"Mom, I don't care what you're marching for. You're making me lose all my friends."

"Stacy, most of our friends were at the rally to support what we're doing. Sarah and Jacob and their mothers were there. Aren't they your best friends? Josh, I'm sorry, Janeen, was there in a short skirt and boots, plus a large group of our temple friends. I let you to stay home. What friends are you talking about?"

"I have other friends, too, Mom. Not everyone thinks like you do. I hate you. Why do you always have to cause trouble? Can't you just let things be?"

Babs' husband, Mark, popped his head into the room.

"Hey, Stacy honey, aren't you late for school? Do you want a ride?"

Stacy put on her cutest smile and rolled her green eyes at her dad. As she quickly dressed and took off with her father, Babs wasn't pleased at all. She looked around the room at the white furniture, powder blue walls, pink bedspread, cabinets full of books, toys, stuffed animals, a closet full of cute outfits, a TV, and a computer. Whatever her baby wanted, Babs provided, and in that moment, it felt like all she received back was complaints and insults.

"I hate you" sure doesn't feel too good.

Stacy had refused to join Babs and Lori at the rally in downtown Chicago. As usual, she whined and maneuvered her way out of doing something she didn't want to do.

That May, people joined rallies across the country, triggered by the leak of a Supreme Court draft to overturn Roe v. Wade. Babs had left it up to her daughters whether to join her. She had hated going to marches with her mother while growing up and she could understand Stacy's reluctance. Still, she didn't expect such a hostile reaction from her own daughter.

Shirley and "The Girls" were there, too. She made quite an expression at her age, striding around in high heels. There were as many men as women. The anti-choice side also had a mix of men and women, which made the question of choice appear to be much more significant than just an issue limited to the women's movement.

Abortion affects men as much as women, whether people like it or not.

That's how Babs explained it to Lori as they drove to the rally.

"It's always been a movement for equality in reproductive rights. In today's world, we rally for all kinds of human rights for all kinds of people—black, white, indigenous, bisexual, nonbinary, trans—you name it, we march to support it. My mother would be lost in today's world with its new language. I even have a hard time keeping up with it, but you and your friends understood it all, don't you?"

Lori shrugged.

"Maybe, Mom, but I don't know that much about how fast these groups could lose their rights, including the right to exist, or what people like my grandmother went through to guarantee them for you and me. I mean, what they had to deal with was crazy!"

Instead of going to the rally, Stacy went out to breakfast with her dad at the Midwest Cafe, a cute little place with flowers everywhere, from the wallpaper to the blue China vases on the wooden tables. They enjoyed strawberry crepes and conversations about her school, his new bikes, and Mom. After greeting a few friends, Mark sat down across from Stacy.

"Stace, I agree with you, Mom gets us into too many controversies, but she is passionate about her ideas. If you can't support her, keep quiet as I do."

Most of their Lake Forest neighbors were conservative. Babs met her husband at one of her paternal grandmother's parties. Mark wasn't Jewish, but he had agreed to let her raise their children in her faith. A rabbi and a priest had married them.

Mark wasn't happy about her and Lori going to the rally.

"I would rather you and Lori stay home and support the cause in other ways. Chicago is no longer safe, you know, between the shootings and the burglaries that are happening everywhere these days. There's crime everywhere, Babs, even here in our suburbs."

Babs hadn't said much at all. She knew it would be futile, that Mark would give in if she didn't agitate.

Old news. That can never keep us off the streets.

Mark wasn't satisfied, however.

"A rally for or against abortion could easily attract some nut with a gun. Listen, Babs, I'm pleading with you to stay home, and Lori, too."

Mark was a quiet conservative who watched Fox News, while Babs tuned into MSNBC. Somehow, despite these differences, they had fallen in love.

Chicago's rising crime rate was not the main thing bothering Mark. He and Babs grew up on different sides of the abortion issue. Chemistry brought Mark and Babs together when they were young. Even today, when he reached for her in bed, her body still tingled. They usually could deal with their differences.

I hope this one won't become the ultimate test.

Most of the people at the rally worried about violence, but they didn't let it stop them from coming. Crime in many major cities had increased, and the Chicago police department was out in full force. Fortunately, nothing terrible happened.

Lieutenant Governor Juliana Stratton said the rally was about economic and racial justice as much as abortion rights. She explained how the poor would have a hard time traveling to a state that allowed abortion and that they would not be able to afford one unless it was paid for by the government or private insurance. She told the crowd that abortion should be safe, legal, and accessible, and that it was up to them to protest the Supreme Court's latest drift to the right. Illinois was still a state that supported abortion, but the number would soon be dwindling. If Roe was overturned, at least twenty states would adopt anti-abortion laws, and everyone knew it would happen fast.

Lori listened carefully to the speeches, especially Stratton's.

"Mom, wasn't that what Shirley said about the original goal back in 1973? You were right when you said we can't let them send us back fifty years."

She grabbed one of the posters being given out and marched with the younger crowd.

Going home was a nightmare. Before Covid, Babs went into the city three or four times a month to go to the theater, shop, and meet friends for lunch or dinner. Now, she hardly left the comfort of her suburban enclave to venture into the city. Between traffic, carjackings, and robberies, everyone was worried, which was a real shame because Chicago, situated on Lake Michigan, was a beautiful city with so much to do.

Babs missed seeing live theater, and new exhibits at the Museum of Science and Industry, the Art Institute, and the Shedd Aquarium.

She continued to keep abreast of the news. So far, the Supreme Court leaker hadn't been found, and the official ruling on Roe v. Wade wouldn't come for several months.

The writing is on the wall, and we've got to do something!

Chapter Three

Monday morning was typically chaotic, but everyone made it out of the house on time. The girls traipsed off to school and Mark headed to work. Babs grabbed her car keys and went to the garage. As she backed out onto the street, she noted the perfect, baby blue spring sky and headed toward Highway 41. She turned south onto the section of Sheridan Road where the North Shore wealthy lived, and finally pulled into the driveway of her destination.

She was right on time her weekly commitment, which was getting harder to deal with each time she went. A quarter of a mile later, her father's mansion became visible. The path uphill on multi-colored stones was surrounded by shiny, emerald-green grass and perfectly trimmed shrubbery, along with clusters of flowers in a rainbow of colors.

Babs parked in front of the two-story red-brick house with a patio and a pool facing Lake Michigan. The atmosphere reminded her of the television series *Downton Abbey*. Her mom and dad bought the house in 1972, and Babs grew up there until she was ten. Her memories were not good. After her parents' divorce, her dad kept the house even though he had a sizable condo in downtown Chicago and a townhouse in London.

She used the big, golden lions-head knocker on the mahogany double door, the same one she loved using as a kid. Dorothy, the gray-haired housekeeper, appeared in a well-starched navy blue and white uniform, with comfortable matching shoes.

"Hello, Dorothy. How is he today?"

"About the same."

"Has my brother been here, or has he contacted our father?"

"He was here about a month ago, but a young man came around twice this week asking, almost insisting, to see your father. He wanted to talk to whoever was in charge. Charles told him he was Mr. Green's caregiver and that no one could see your father without your permission."

"Did he leave a card or give you a name or a reason?"

"No, he never did. I never saw him before, and I've been here twenty years. He's about your age, tall with sandy-colored hair. He spoke with a slight accent and drove a small, white rented car."

"My father worked worldwide, Dorothy. He could be a friend or a journalist. If the young man comes around again, don't let him in, but give him my phone number."

Babs walked through the white-and-tan marble foyer, past the Chagall and Picasso paintings, past the lush, tan carpeted front room with the oversized off-white sofas with gold tasseled pillows, and through the patio doors to the white, Italian tiled patio with its three enormous flagstone tables and white and blue-striped canvas umbrellas. Even though the house hadn't been remodeled in 20 years, it still looked like it was being staged for a showing.

Babs remembered a terrible scene when her brother spilled red pasta on the light carpet. Her mother shuffled them out of the house before Dad threatened to kill her brother. Material possessions were important to him, and he never tolerated accidents, even by his own children.

Charles looked as dapper as ever in his black chauffeur's uniform. He slowly stood up and brought Babs a comfortable and plush lounge chair, which he placed next to her father's wheelchair. After being his chauffeur for many years, Charles was now her father's caretaker.

"Good morning, Babs. Coffee?"

"Yes, please. You know I can't live without it."

Babs moved in front of her father and bent down to greet him.

"Hello, Dad. It's Babs, your daughter."

Ronnie stared at her as he grasped the brown, cashmere throw she had brought him last week. She sat down next to him. Some days he knew her; some days he just stared; and other times, he called her Sherrie. That was odd because she was about five inches taller than her mother, and she wore her brown and blonde-streaked hair straight. Her mother was barely five feet tall and had thick, black wavy hair. Babs remembered the terrible crying and angry outbursts, but at least her father knew who she was during that time.

He's like an empty shell now.

Alzheimer's is tough for anyone to deal with, and now it was Babs' job to do the best she could. Her dad had enjoyed a million girlfriends, but he had never remarried or had any other children besides Babs and her brother, Jim. His only sibling, a sister, had died. Her children had never been around, though, at least not up to that point.

They probably will show up at the reading of the will.

Babs and Jim had joint power of attorney, so they would have to eventually talk when it came to matters concerning their father. Their thinking was poles apart. Babs needed Jim's okay on everything she was doing to keep her father alive. Larry, his long-time lawyer and friend, allowed them to sell the condo, but not the townhouse in London. The money from the sale was used for his care. So far, there were no treatments to stop or reverse the disease. Larry had found a top specialist to treat Ronnie, and Babs had checked all leads concerning new medications.

During the last doctor's visit, Babs realized how bad her father had become when he didn't flirt with the new, young blonde nurse. The doctor shook his head sadly when he confirmed Babs' worst suspicions.

"I'm sorry, Babs, but he seems to be sliding away faster than we thought. Last month, he could give me responses. Today, he doesn't know me."

Dorothy entered with a cup of black coffee and a plate of oatmeal cookies. She and Charles left her alone with her father. Babs took a sip of the coffee and a bite of a cookie. When she offered one to her father, he pushed her hand away. As she tried to get him to talk to her, she noticed that he was losing weight.

Babs nervously twirled a lock of hair around her fingers.

I wonder how Mom would feel about the care I'm giving to Dad.

Her mother loved and hated her father. Dad was a womanizer, and a dictator at home. Before the divorce, he was tough to live with, but afterward, he was there for Babs and her brother. Babs remembered those as good days, while Jim only remembered them as bad. He was still carrying a tremendous grudge.

A half-hour later, with no response from her father, Babs got up to leave. She found Charles and Dorothy in the ultra-modern kitchen with custom cabinets, new digital appliances, and granite everywhere. She doubted that Dorothy ever cooked in that space. She was a traditional housekeeper in her late sixties. Her husband, Charles, immediately returned to the patio to look after Ronnie.

A month earlier, when her father was more responsive, he had wandered away from the mansion. After Charles finally found him walking down Sheridan Road, he never left him alone again. He and Dorothy had been tried-and-true, faithful employees of Dad's for years. Babs remembered once hiding from her father behind the steps leading down to the beach. She didn't remember why. Her father scared her when they lived with him. Now, he was changing so fast that it frightened her in much different way.

"Charles, do you or Dorothy need anything? If not, I will be back next Monday."

She knew Charles had access to the one remaining car from her dad's collection of English autos. He loved that seven-year-old Bentley. Babs stopped inside a restroom before leaving. She stepped out of one sandal and touched the floor with her foot to see if the tile was still heated.

One more thing on my list for the next time Mark and I do some remodeling.

Babs stood outside for a few minutes, taking in the beautiful surroundings. She thought about how keeping this house would cost a fortune, but when Dad gave Jim and her power of attorney, he specified that the Glencoe house couldn't be sold until he died. Jim wanted to put him in a special facility for Alzheimer's patients and close the house once and for all. Babs couldn't do that to her father. He was a proud, arrogant man who had held prominent positions in Republican administrations. She had to keep his illness a secret and let him live out his days in peace because she knew how horrified he would be if people saw him as weak and failing.

That's his ego talking to the very end.

His doctors said he had only about one year left. Maybe less. Babs went to all her father's medical appointments in addition to her vising each Monday.

Babs opened the car door, slipped on her sunglasses, and took off. Halfway down the driveway, a thought came to her. She stopped the car and called Dorothy.

"Dorothy, my father put cameras everywhere. If you find a picture of the young man who bothered you, have Charles e-mail it to me."

The young man looking for Dad is probably a journalist.

Chapter Four

Mark was at a meeting after work and Lori had basketball practice. Babs stopped by the local grocery store. It felt good to shop without a mask. They were voluntary now, and schools and most other activities had gone live instead of on Zoom. Covid was still around, but more like the flu than a death sentence.

After two years of that terrible pandemic, things are finally returning to normal.

In 2021, Lori and Mark had come down with Covid, but not Stacy or Babs.

We were both too mean!

They all had vaccinations and boosters, which were supposed to protect them. Poor Mark was as sick as a dog for two weeks. Babs was afraid he would end up in the hospital. They were all quarantined the entire time.

Keeping them away from each other, feeding them, shopping, and cleaning had been a nightmare for Babs. The worst of it was that Vicky, her cleaning lady, wasn't allowed in the house. Mark and Lori complained about missing work, and Stacy couldn't understand why she had to be quarantined if she wasn't sick.

As Babs walked around the grocery store, she was surprised at the rise in prices and the many empty shelves. Stacy had complained that The Dollar Store should now be called The Dollar and a Quarter Store. Babs had hardly slept the night before, worried about her father and the situation with her brother, and she yawned as she pushed her cart. She decided to take the easy way out and buy ready-made fried chicken and all the fixings. It was Stacy's favorite, anyway, so she wouldn't need to worry about any complaints on that front.

We Won't Go Back

Babs pulled into the garage, careful to move around the many bicycles. Mark was a pack rat, which meant she was constantly making trips to Goodwill. Babs found Stacy lying across their purple couch, watching a Netflix movie. She sat down beside her.

"How was school?"

"Great. Everyone forgot about the rally. We are too busy concentrating on our eighth-grade promotion, which will be late this year, but in person instead of on Zoom, thank God."

"I brought home a roasted chicken. It's just you and me, Honey."

"Great, Mom. This movie will be over in fifteen minutes."

"What are you watching?"

"Crazy Rich Asians."

"Is that the one where they play mahjong? Aunt Tillie tried to teach me, but I'm not a game person. I bet you would like it."

"I like all games, Mom. I play dominoes. That's with tiles, too."

Babs went into the kitchen to put away her groceries. She was tempted to approach Stacy about her attitude toward the rally but thought better of it. She didn't want to risk turning a nice moment into another conflict. Still, she was frustrated by the overall lack of support for a cause she held near and dear to her heart.

Everyone forgot about the rally. Shirley was right when she said if we don't keep the heat up, everyone will forget. This generation has no idea how hard so many women worked 50 years ago to get Roe v. Wade passed.

Babs had a meeting coming on Thursday. She imagined her mother, Sherrie, and Ruth Bader Ginsburg, crying together somewhere up in heaven. Maybe they were lamenting the fact that their once beloved country had become so divided.

All the news is tainted to one extreme or the other.

Babs often switched between Fox and MSNBC, just to see the different coverage of the same event, and then settled on a British or Israeli station to get simple, factual real-world news.

She remembered her mother saying at her wedding that a Democratic judge and a Republican senator sat together, talking, and laughing. Babs wondered if that could still happen, and what kind of world her daughters would live in when they became mothers.

She and Stacy ate chicken, potato salad, and biscuits. They ignored the tumult of the day and discussed promotion activities. Stacy's graduating class would be the first one in two years to have a live promotion instead of celebrating on Zoom.

As Babs listened to her daughter, she couldn't quite let go of her frustration over Stacy's immature and selfish response to the abortion issue. To Babs, Stacy only cared about being popular, and was ignoring a much bigger issue that all women and girls should consider.

"Stacy, I'm still troubled about your response to my participation in the rally and the fight for a woman's right to choose. This affects you too, you know! Maybe not today, or this year, and I certainly hope it won't matter in your personal life for a long time, but what about women in general?"

"What about them, Mom?"

"Stacy, we are *not* baby killers! We are fighting for women to have a choice in whether they keep a child or abort it."

"Mom, I really don't care. I just don't want my friends to leave me out of their group."

"Really? Is that the only thing that's important to you?"

"Uh, yeah, right now, for sure it is."

Babs cleared the table and took a deep breath.

I can't deal with any more conflict right now.

"Okay, Stacy, let's save this discussion for another day."

"Good idea, Mom. By the way, I need a new dress for promotion." Babs did her best to go with the flow.

"Won't you be in cap and gown?"

"Afterwards, yeah, and for the school dance that night. Can we go shopping tomorrow? Some of my friends will be in the mall."

Babs checked the wall calendar. Rummage sale at the Temple.

I can miss that.

As she cleaned up from dinner, she called out from the kitchen.

"It's a date, Stacy! Tomorrow morning."

Chapter Five

Babs showered, brushed her teeth, and threw on a pair of jeans and a short-sleeve pink top. Before rushing out of the house, she opened Stacy's door.

"I forgot about my hair appointment. I'll pick you up at eleven to go dress shopping."

Her usual Friday appointment had been changed by her beautician to Saturday.

"Mom, you have to put your calendar on your phone, not on the wall."

Mark and Lori were already at the breakfast table.

"Lori, you can join us shopping."

"No way, Mom. Anyway, I have basketball practice."

Babs grabbed Mark's cream-cheese bagel and raced to her car, thinking that if it were not for people like her mother and Shirley, her daughter would never be allowed to play basketball.

Doesn't anyone remember Title IX? What are they teaching our kids in school?

Babs realized that if Lori's boyfriend wasn't on the boys' team, she probably would have never thought of joining the girls' team.

We women have come so far, yet some things will always be the same.

Lassie, tail wagging, came running after her.

"Would somebody please feed the dog? I'm late!"

Lassie was Babs' fourth collie, all descended from her first. She was a collie person from the time she was 13 and won out over her brother who wanted a cat. Truthfully, her obsession with collies began from the time she saw Elizabeth Taylor in *Courage of Lassie*.

We Won't Go Back

The small, four-chair beauty shop was located just a few minutes away, next to a cute family-owned restaurant in downtown Lake Forest. Kelly, the owner, was waiting for Babs when she arrived. "Sorry I'm late. Between Stacy's promotion and my involvement with the movement, I can't keep my schedule straight. Can you believe Roe v. Wade could be overturned after all this time?"

Kelly, normally friendly and talkative, didn't say a word and her face went blank. Babs turned back over her shoulder to see what was wrong.

"Mrs. Wood, I've been doing your hair for almost twenty years, right?"

Babs nodded.

"Please let's not talk politics. My beliefs are different than yours."

Babs felt uncomfortable as soon as she heard what Kelly said. The next hour was awkward for both women. Instead of their usual non-stop chatter on any number of subjects, neither one said a word. Even Julie, the nail girl, kept her voice to a whisper. It was as if the words "Roe" and "Wade" made the beauty shop go quiet.

On the way home, Babs realized why Stacy was so angry. After all, a photograph of Babs had appeared in the newspaper the day after the rally. She wasn't sure if she could go back to the beauty shop or if she would even be welcome. Her cut, color, and blow-dry were perfect.

Kelly is talented and I like her, but . . .

Babs called Stacy to let her know she would pick her up in a few minutes. Naturally, Stacy wasn't quite ready when her mother pulled into the driveway, so Babs waited in the car with the air conditioning on, checking her messages and e-mail. She was way behind on playing her favorite word game, but her friends would understand. Ninety degree-days. Crazy Chicago weather for May. Babs hadn't even taken out her summer clothes. She was wearing her trusted jeans and a short-sleeve, blue, Eileen Fisher top.

Ten minutes later, Stacy appeared in her fashionable jeans with holes in them.

Amazing how the fashion world can sell anything.

Stacy had her hair up in a ponytail. It needed cutting, but now Babs was afraid to return to the beauty shop.

I could just drop off Stacy and keep a low profile.

Stacy opened the passenger door, slid into the car, and buckled up.

"Mom, your hair looks great. I like the blonde highlights."

"Thanks. They aren't too blonde, are they?"

"No, You look sexy. Dad will like it."

Where do they get these ideas?

Babs backed out of the driveway.

"Where to?"

"Urban Outfitters."

"We'll start there, but a department store might be better for a dance dress."

They walked out of Urban Outfitters with some cute tops, but no dress, so they drove on to the mall with the music of one of the K-pop groups blasting on the radio. Stacy's eyes never left her phone. After parking, Babs recorded "2C" on her phone so they wouldn't forget where the car was on the way back. Most of the cars were luxury vehicles since they were in a North Shore suburb. Babs reached inside for her sweater. Stacy shook her head.

"Mom, it's ninety degrees and you're taking a sweater."

"It's not hot in the air-conditioned stores, and you know I always get cold."

The mall was relatively empty for a Saturday afternoon. Inflation, online shopping, and the lack of available merchandise were the problems. They took the elevator up to the second floor and entered Macy's, which seemed to be the only busy store.

A young sales lady in a short, flowered dress, approached them.

"Are you looking for a prom dress? They are twenty percent off this weekend and there is a run on them."

Babs and Stacy followed the salesgirl to the teen department, which offered racks of dresses. Stacy left Babs and the girl alone while she ran over to greet a friend.

"Hi Britany, did you find anything?"

The salesgirl smiled at Babs.

"It's been like this all morning. What is your daughter's favorite color?"

"She likes pink and blues."

"I think she is probably a two. Take her to the dressing room. I'll pick out some things."

As Babs went to get Stacy, she took out a tissue and wiped her face. She didn't need a sweater because the store was unusually hot.

I doubt the air conditioner is even on.

Macy's wasn't her favorite, but they had a good teen department.

The dressing room was hot, small, and noisy. Babs was getting a headache. After Stacy tried on about six different dresses, Babs was ready to leave. Stacy admired herself in the mirror.

"I love it."

She gazed at a thin-strapped, white lace dress over a silk undergarment.

Too short for my taste, but Stacy looks cute.

One hundred and fifty dollars later they were seated in The Claim Company for lunch. It was a traditional restaurant from the '60s with a Southwestern gold mining theme, featuring dark wood-paneled walls, wooden covered-wagon lights, and brown vinyl booths.

"Mom, The Claim Company used to be my favorite restaurant because of the salad bar. Why did they close it?"

"Covid. All salad bars were closed, and many of restaurants, too."

Help wanted signs were everywhere. Babs sat down, put a napkin on her lap, and opened the menu, which was much smaller than before.

"Stacy, their famous hamburger on black bread is still on the menu."

"Okay, I guess I'll have the hamburger. It was always good. I hate that everything is changing due to this stupid Covid. When will we be normal again?"

"Don't be so pessimistic. We've had a good day shopping, and things are easing. Masks are now voluntary instead of mandatory, and we can now go to malls and restaurants."

Stacy hates change, and it's been a tough two years for her.

"Thanks for the dress, Mom."

Stacy took out her cell phone. Babs opened hers, too, and texted her daughter.

"Hi Stacy, can we talk face to face sometimes?"

Stacy looked up.

"Okay, Mom. What do you want to talk about?"

"Anything. Just put away your phone."

That worked until their food was served, and Stacy's phone vibrated. At the same time, Babs got a picture from Dorothy, which she showed to Stacy.

"Honey, this guy is stalking your grandpa's house. I've never seen him before. I bet he is a reporter."

Stacy took the phone and looked at the ring picture.

"He's cute. I like his dimples, but not his clothes."

The stranger was dressed in a weird, camel hair cardigan sweater over tan trousers. Too conservative for his age.

We Won't Go Back

The waitress cleared the table and asked if they wanted anything else.

"Just the check, please."

"Mom, what about their famous fudge brownie a la mode?"

"You have room? You ate the whole burger and half the fries."

The waitress stood still and smiled. This was a routine she had observed often. Babs looked up and smiled back.

"We will have the brownie and then the check."

While Stacy ate the fudge brownie, Babs texted her brother.

"Jim, I need to talk to you."

To her surprise, he answered immediately.

"If Ronnie died, I'll talk."

Jim never called their father "Father" or "Dad," only "Ronnie," the same as her mother did. He never told her why.

Babs sent Jim the picture and asked if he recognized the person. She soon realized that he was back to not answering. Stacy looked at the phone.

"Do you have a picture of Uncle Jim? I haven't seen him in five years. He didn't even come to my Bat Mitzvah."

Babs sighed and looked for the message telling her where she had left the car so she could avoid talking about her brother.

"Mom, the car is in 2C. You can stop looking already. Oh, and the keys are at the bottom of your purse, but you don't need them. Just push the button."

Babs stared at Stacy and thought better of snapping at her. They'd had a nice time shopping and she didn't want to ruin the moment.

I know I have a hard time understanding all this new equipment, but my daughter does not need to treat me like an idiot.

"Okay, Stacy, thank you for explaining all of that."

"Sure, Mom. Whatever."

On the way home, they stopped at a gas station. Babs was shocked when she saw the price: $5.00 a gallon. Mark had been filling up their car and she hadn't realized how much prices had gone up. Covid seemed to be over, but getting back to living normally presented all kinds of roadblocks: rising prices for food and gas and who knows what else, escalating crime, the stock market dropping, and a war in Ukraine.

In Babs' mind, the worst situation was about to unfold when the Supreme Court ruled on abortion rights.

We haven't seen the worst of it yet, for sure.

Chapter Six

On Saturday morning, Babs dressed in jeans, a blue v-neckline top, and sandals. She entered the kitchen, where the family was already eating breakfast.

"Who wants to go with me to see Papa? I need to see if he recognizes the man who has been stalking his house. Dorothy sent a picture yesterday of the guy on their patio."

Mark looked up from his newspaper.

"What is with you and that guy? Your dad is out of it, and the man is probably a reporter. *The Wall Street Journal* had a piece, asking, 'Where is Judge Green? Why hasn't he been interviewed about the abortion laws?'"

Babs was not sure how to respond to Mark.

It's too early to discuss abortion.

"Sometimes Dad remembers things from the past. He could know him."

"I'll go," said Lori.

"Not me," Stacy said.

She poured herself some orange juice.

"He scared me, even when he was well."

Stacy was her father's girl. If she had a chance to be with Mark, she would stay and help him with whatever he was up to or talk him into taking her somewhere she wanted to go.

Lori grabbed her purse, gulped down the rest of her orange juice, and followed her mother to the car. Babs adjusted her seat belt, turned the engine on, and then stopped.

"What's wrong, Mom?"

"I left some flowers on the patio. That house is so cold and sterile that I thought I'd bring flowers to cheer my father up. I got your dad to let go of some his beauties from the garden."

"I'll get them," Lori said.

Once she retrieved the flowers, they were on their way. It didn't take long before Babs questioned Lori about her boyfriend.

"So, where is Josh? I haven't seen him lately."

Lori blushed.

"He's still around, but he's working and playing basketball. He needs to keep his college scholarship."

Babs nodded.

"Makes sense."

"Mom, I think I am in love with him."

Seventeen, and she is in love. Be careful with your answers, Babs.

She made sure to temper her response.

"That's great, but you are a little young to be in love, don't you think? We all like Josh. Going to college will be the test of time for both of you."

They continued to talk about Josh, college, and Lori's senior year of high school. Babs stopped the car in front of her father's house.

"Mom, it must have been heaven to grow up in this gorgeous mansion."

"Not exactly, Lori. My father was so strict and unpredictable. I was scared to death of shattering or ruining anything in the house. And you know, the pool, the patio, the fountains, and the back addition came after the divorce. I know every nook and cranny in the front part of the house because I hid in them when Dad came home. We never knew if he would be mean or nice. My brother loved to pull me out of hiding. I couldn't stand it when he did that. You know, Lori, money and luxury things don't always make you happy."

Lori stared at her mother.

"It's hard to believe the stories you tell about Papa. He was always good to me, and he bought me all those expensive presents from countries he visited or worked in. I put them away in my closet. I especially like the egg from Russia."

"He was good with the gifts as long as you remembered to do what he demanded."

"Mom, you are being mean.

Babs rolled her eyes.

"Will he ever get better?"

"Not unless they find new medicines, or a cure."

"How did you know he has Alzheimer's?"

"The only way to be sure used to be to look at your brain after death, like with a cat scan, but now the doctors can pretty much tell from your behavior. After Dad retired, he lived alone so it took a while. One of the signs was mood changes, but he always had those. One of his girlfriends called me once and said, 'Something is wrong with your father. He doesn't remember anything, and he gets mean. I'm getting out of here.' It took almost another year before Dad let us help him. By us, I mean his partner and best friend, Larry Eltin, and me."

"What about Dorothy and Charles? Did they see anything different?"

"This happened about three years ago when Dad spent most of his time in the condo downtown. H used the house mainly for entertaining or getting away to rest."

As they drove up the long driveway, they heard the noise of a tractor and breathed in the aroma of fresh-cut grass and the hint of lilac blooms.

Dorothy opened the front door.

"Nice to see you, Lori. Your grandfather is in the dining room, and he seems pretty good today. He ate a little and responded to Charles with several words."

As they walked through the house to the dining room, Babs wondered why her father never had any family pictures up on the walls or on a table or the piano. Nothing. She had so few pictures of him, but tons of her mom's family, especially from when they lived in their famous family building in one of Chicago's old Jewish neighborhoods.

Lori looked around the den with its wooden, built-in ceiling-to-floor bookshelves.

"Mom, did your dad read all these books?"

Most of them were hard-covered classics.

"Do you think I could borrow some?"

"Of course, you can. I bet your grandfather never read any of them. He only read non-fiction, like *The New York Times,* and law books. If I remember correctly a designer put the books on the shelves to make the room look classy."

The extra-high ceiling made the bookshelves look like they belonged in a law library. Lori, the most ambitious reader in the family, took two old classics: *The Great Gatsby* and *Farewell to Arms.*

Babs took note of her selections.

"F. Scott Fitzgerald and Ernest Hemingway. Impressive."

Lori rolled her eyes.

"Thanks, Mom."

They moved into the dining room, where Babs stared at the emaciated old man in a wheelchair. Her father was deteriorating every day. She realized that Jim might have been correct when he recently assessed the situation in one of the few times he conversed with Babs.

"You like having power over him, Babs. That's why you visit him so much. I will only be happy when he is dead."

Babs remembered her father and Jim screaming at each other, which often ended in Jim getting a beating. Her father never physically touched her, but he did scare her. She and her mother lived with constant fear and anxiety.

Before she could try to talk to her father, he reached out to Lori, who moved close to him. As he held his granddaughter's hand, he surprised everyone when he spoke.

"Babs, you've finally come to visit."

Lori looked at her mother, not sure how to respond.

"Just play along," Babs whispered. "Show him the picture and ask if he knows the man."

Babs stepped back and let Lori question her grandfather.

Ronnie threw the picture on the floor, put his hands in the air, shook his head back and forth, and began to yell.

"No! No! No, you can't marry him!"

Then, Ronnie tried to hit Lori. Charles rushed over to calm him down. Babs felt her heart pound. During the last year, she had never seen her father so agitated.

As Lori and Babs went into the hallway, Charles followed them.

"He needs to rest now. Come back soon on another day."

Lori was visibly shaken.

"What happened?" she said. "Did I do something wrong?"

"I'm not sure," said Charles. "Alzheimer's is such a mysterious disease. Sometimes, his memory makes him act out, or maybe it's because he can't express himself the way he wants and gets terribly frustrated. I'm not sure. No one is, really. It isn't your fault, Lori."

Babs wasn't happy about taking Lori home on such a bad note.

"Let's go for some ice cream."

They drove down Sheridan Road, with its glamorous old mansions and ancient trees with overhanging branches, until they found a Dairy Queen.

They sat down on a worn bench and sipped at their shakes.

"Mom, do you think Papa knew the man in the picture?"

Babs shrugged.

"Who knows? Alzheimer's is a terrible disease. We are lucky to have Charles and Dorothy. Most victims at this stage end up entering a special facility. That would be so unpleasant for him and all of us, too."

Babs's phone rang. She dug into her oversized purse until she found it.

"Oh my gosh. Sorry, Mark. I forgot about the graduation party for your nephew. We're on our way home."

She looked at Lori.

"Sometimes I forget that your father has a family, too. Let's move."

Chapter Seven

Since the Supreme Court news broke on abortion rights, Babs had been distracted and wanted to make sure she was taking adequate care of her family. She left a note on the fridge about a spaghetti and salad dinner being ready for dinner and a reminder that she was going to a meeting at Shirley's.

Ducks in a row. Here I go.

The sky thickened as she drove down the expressway. A combination of rain and sleet pinged against her windows. She was driving into the city at three o'clock in the afternoon when traffic should have been going the other way. That was not happening today. She moved into the right lane to avoid speeding drivers. To make things worse, some crazy bicyclist bumped into her car when she got off at Ohio Street. She pulled over and got out of the car, wrestling with an umbrella as she made sure all was well.

Thank God he isn't hurt.

Babs offered the man money and her umbrella, but he just wanted to escape. He jumped back onto his bike and sped away in the rain. She continued to Shirley's place and gave her car keys to the doorman. She glanced at the side of the car and saw a scratch from the bicycle.

Mark will not be happy, but it's my car, not his.

Between the weather and the age of Shirley's group, there were only eight people at the meeting. This time, Babs dressed in a floral cotton dress instead of her tried-and-true blue jeans. As usual, she was the youngest one in the group. She felt like a representative for her mother, especially when Shirley took out a massive poster that she and Babs's mother had made for a 1973 rally in Washington, D.C Rally.

EQUALITY OF RIGHTS UNDER THE LAW SHALL
NOT BE DENIED OR ABRIDGED
BY THE UNITED STATES OR ANY STATE ON
ACCOUNT OF SEX.

Mom had good handwriting!

The group discussed all sorts of problems that could arise if the law was reversed. Organizing peaceful rallies, how to handle the fear of terrorists on both sides, lobbying for a national referendum and vote, debating if the Democratic Congress could pass a federal law, making abortion legal, how losing the fight over Roe v. Wade could affect other women's rights, the ramifications for in-vitro fertilization, birth control, over-the-counter abortion pills, medicated abortions, and even gay marriage.

Linda raised her hand. Shirley looked at her and frowned.

"We're not in school. Just talk."

"Shirley, you talk so fast it's hard to get in the conversation."

There was a quiet giggle and nods from the other women. Shirley raised her eyebrows.

"Is that what you wanted to say?"

Linda gestured in protest.

"No, no. I wanted to point out that Nancy Pelosi is a Catholic like I am, and she says *every* woman has the right to choose."

After some heated discussion, Shirley looked up at her friends and asked them to hush.

"Listen, everyone, I am very concerned about reports that a group calling themselves Jane's Revenge was engaged in a terrorist activity. They seem to have claimed responsibility for an attack on a pro-life center in Asheville. Three of us in this room were part of the original Jane in Chicago, and we didn't then and would never now engage in terror tactics. Our goal was to provide a safe, clean, free, or reasonable place for women who needed counseling, emotional support, or an abortion. Back in 1970, women with money paid up to a thousand dollars for illegal abortions. We were middle-class women in our twenties to forties helping women who had no place to go. When a woman needed an abortion, she would call a specific number and ask for Jane. We left the numbers to call at hospitals, stores, clinics, and colleges. Jane's Revenge started in Chicago in 1968 and operated in the shadows until Roe v. Wade become the law of the land. We were aggressive when we had to be, but never violent. We need to find out who is using our name."

"Amen."

The response was uniform.

Babs twirled a piece of hair around her finger.

"Shirley, my mom was a Jane, right?"

Shirley hesitated, but Eleanor jumped in.

"Sherrie was an unofficial Jane. She helped direct patients to the official Janes. She answered calls, and she drove women to the houses. When she was twenty, Sherry's roommate had a botched abortion, and Sherrie refused to be in any operating rooms with us."

Shirley smiled.

"I first gave your mom a job with abused women and then doing financial seminars. She was great at both. Our goal was to make women aware of their family's financial world. At that time, men were dying in Vietnam, leaving their widows ignorant of where to get money and how to pay their bills. It's so different now, Babs. I bet you are the one paying bills and investing in your household."

Babs rearranged her skirt and took a drink from her coffee cup.

"I remember that. I helped Mom do seminars. She made me learn things, like balancing a checkbook and dealing with the bills and the stock market, and how to do insurance. My husband hates paperwork, so it works out for us. I remember that my mom worked with someone named Denice, who kept cracking her knuckles."

Shirley laughed.

"Denice was smart, but she was afraid of her shadow. I think she gave up law, got married, and had four kids."

Eleanor patted Babs on the back.

"Your mom was a sweetheart. One of the nicest people I ever knew. After making it as a lawyer in the big world, she still had that small close family way about her. She died too young."

"Thank you," Babs said.

She couldn't speak. She hurried into the bathroom, where she let the tears flow. Her mom had died of lung cancer at the age of 48 and Babs was just a little past that now. She missed her mom's kind heart, her smile, her touch, the smell of her Chanel No. 5 perfume, and her Jewish cooking. She also remembered the endless blood tests until there were no veins left to tap, oxygen masks, clumps of black hair laying on her pillow, and at the end, her skeleton body gasping for breath.

Babs was in her early 20s when her mother died. She missed her, but after 25 years, she had come to terms with the fact that life goes on, no matter what. Now, with Roe v. Wade in the news again, Babs thought about her mother daily. In her ride home from Shirley's, she struggled to drive through her tears and anger. She turned off the radio, hoping the silence would ease her troubled heart.

My mother was much more passionate about causes then me. While Mom and Shirley were leaders in the fight for women's rights, I am a follower, but a good one!

Back in the garage, Babs smelled sweaty socks and spilled red wine. Inside the house, she heard a marching sound. When she followed the noise to her front room, she saw Mark, dressed in blue athletic shorts and a wrinkled University of Illinois t-shirt, pacing back and forth. He looked haggard, and he was holding a drink in his hand.

Babs was befuddled.

"Mark! What is wrong? Did something happen to the girls?"

"No, they are fine. You and I need to talk."

He gulped his drink.

"Mark! Stop pacing and sit down."

Babs reached for his glass and looked in it.

"What are you drinking? Smells like alcohol."

"I tried red wine, but Jack and Coke work better."

He smiled.

Babs became anxious. Mark was low-key, and he usually worked things out without getting so upset.

Is he sick? Did he lose his job? Does he have a girlfriend?

She sat down on the sofa. Mark remained standing and took another swig of his drink.

"You can't keep going to these rallies and meetings, Babs. It's got to stop. You're putting our lives in danger."

Babs took a deep breath and relaxed her shoulders. She and Mark could deal with the rallies and her involvement with abortion issues.

Something else is going on here.

She looked directly at Mark.

"When we got married, we made a pact that we would allow each other to have different opinions on issues and engage in our activities. Remember, Mark?"

He nodded.

"We were raised differently. I know your religious background makes you support the abortion ban. As much as I disagree, I get it. I can see your mother doing hallelujahs while my mom, if she were alive, would be wailing."

Mark put his drink down and tried to hug her. Babs backed off.

"I'm not talking about our differences, Babs. This whole situation is a bomb ready to be dropped. It isn't like when you marched for equal pay for women. This thing will divide the country and wake up all the nuts. I don't want them coming to our doorstep."

Babs twirled a piece of hair around her finger.

I think I've got a little fight on my hands here.

"Mark, I hear you, but you know where I stand. My mother worked to pass Roe v. Wade fifty years ago. I support everything she and Shirley and all those women did. Women, and women only, should decide what to do with their own bodies. Not some group of men on the Supreme Court or in Congress or in a Statehouse. To me, that's not up for debate. Nope. Not at all. I owe it to my daughters, to my mother, and every woman who needs care. There's no room for discussion on that."

Oh my, I wish Mom could have just heard me. And Lori and Stacy, too.

Mark stepped forward clumsily and tried to hug Babs. His hands were cold and sweaty, and she couldn't ignore how he was moving under the influence.

"Babs, you're making all of us crazy."

She turned away and went upstairs to their bedroom, undressed, brushed her teeth, put on her floral nightgown, and quietly slid under a white comforter. About an hour later, when Mark joined her in bed, she moved away from him and closer to Lassie, who had left Stacy's room and joined her bed, almost like she knew Babs needed her. She cuddled up next to 60 pounds of soft sable and white fur.

We Won't Go Back

I guess we've still got to work through our differences, but not right now.

Chapter Eight

As the alarm clock pinged again, Babs tried to sleep through it. It was Saturday, and the rest of the family were still in bed. When the bright red numbers on her digital clock hit 6:30, she quietly raised herself out of bed. After her fight with Mark, Babs had a hard time sleeping through the night. The sun shined through the window. It was another beautiful, cloudless spring day. She did her morning toiletries, threw on a tan jogging outfit, reheated a cup of coffee from the day before, and headed out the door with Lassie. She had hardly been exercising lately. She paid for a health club membership that she never used.

Clear sky, calm breeze, temperature in the high 60s—perfect.

Songbirds, walkers, and joggers joined her. She felt better as soon as she stepped outside.

Lassie tried to chase a rabbit. It took all of Babs' strength to hang on to the leash. Lassie was a good dog who wouldn't go far, but she was worried about the little bunny. One time, Lassie found a rabbit's nest and brought Babs all four of the babies. When she couldn't find the nest, and the mother never came back, she and the girls tried to take care of them, but they all died. That was their first brush with death, which Babs never forgot.

A neighbor in a robe, holding the morning paper, waved. She waved back. and stopped a minute to catch her breath. That was when she saw the lawn signs in front of two houses. One said STOP KILLING BABIES and the one next door said A WOMAN HAS THE RIGHT TO HER BODY.

Babs stopped cold. She lived in a middle class to upper-middle-class neighborhood where everyone knew each other and seemed mindful of living in a peaceful community. Most people had lived there for more than 20 years.

Maybe Mark is right. Abortion could be the ticking bomb.

Babs hated controversy. With the country already so divided over so many issues, she wondered what would happen the following month when the Supreme Court handed down its decision. So far, the rallies and protests had been peaceful. As she walked home, Babs looked back at the two signs. She imagined what might happen if once friendly neighbors stopped talking to each other and turned a cold shoulder toward her, including one of her own daughters.

Maybe I should slow down with the protests.

As Babs got back to the house and entered the kitchen, she watched Lassie shake herself off and run to her bowl of water. She breathed in the sweet aroma of pancakes sizzling in butter, as Mark busily cooked breakfast. He liked cooking more than she did. He was the one who ordered the new digital electric stove she was still trying to figure out. She had to admit she liked the subzero refrigerator. On top of that, she wanted to replace the pink Formica countertops with granite and re-do the worn floor tiles.

Someday. When women have the right to choose, I will have a new floor.

"Babs! It's banana pancake day! Sit down and join us."

Mark's enthusiasm shook Babs out of her worries, at least for the moment. Stacy and Lori were eating and texting. She sat down and joined them. Mark put a plate of pancakes, syrup, and a cup of coffee in front of her. She looked into his eyes and whispered.

"I'm surprised you are working so well this morning."

He smiled.

Babs turned to her girls,

"What is everyone doing today?"

"Going bowling with Joannie," said Stacy. "Her mother is driving." She went back to her texting.

Mark turned around to face her.

"I'm starting my gardening and taking a bike ride. Care to join me?"

Mark and Babs had made a life together for more than 20 years with little in common. Gardening and biking were never on her weekend to-do list. She had failed at both. First, she bloodied her nose while trying to pick apples when she got hit by a branch, and she had so many mishaps while riding a bike that she'd lost count.

Babs quickly changed the subject.

"Lori, what about you?"

"Josh and I are taking a ride up to his parents' summer home in Lake Geneva."

She conveniently didn't mention that they will be alone.

"Isn't Lake Geneva in Wisconsin?" said Stacy.

"Yeah, what about it?" said Lori. "You trying to show off that you paid attention in geography class?"

"Ha ha. You're so funny."

"Girls," said Mark. "Can you just eat and text without fighting?"

"Sure, Daddy," Stacy said. "Can I have another pancake?"

"Have a good time, Lori, and be careful," Babs said.

Lori and Josh had been going together for almost two years. Babs had tried to talk to Lori about birth control, but she found it difficult. She wasn't naive enough to think they weren't having sex or at least thinking about it.

Josh certainly is. He's a teenage boy!

However, this was not the right time, not in front of Stacy and especially not with Mark around, when the conversation could easily pivot to talking about abortion. Now, just when it was about to be outlawed, Babs was more worried than ever.

We Won't Go Back

I should talk to Shirley about getting that new medical abortion pill, just in case . . .

Chapter Nine

Lori spent the morning trying on different bathing suits. She couldn't decide between a two-piece flowered suit or a one-piece black. She ended up dropping both in her bag. She had dieted all week, and she knew she looked good. She admired herself in the mirror, sure that a pair of cut-off jean shorts and an orange crop top would work for the ride to Lake Geneva. She normally didn't wear makeup, but this morning she put on some eye shadow and soft pink lipstick. She was hoping for some assurance from Josh about their future, now that they knew they would attend different colleges.

Josh picked up Lori by noon. It was a two-hour ride, most by expressway. The pretty part started at Highway 12, but so did the traffic. It took them 20 minutes to get through Richmond, Illinois, a town that had once been famous for antiques. Now that no one was interested anymore, it became a famous restaurant town. Josh loved his convertible, but he reluctantly put the top up when Lori said she was worried about her hair. As he pushed the button and let the mechanics do their thing, he mumbled to himself.

"I don't understand girls."

Lori heard him and burst out laughing.

"For sure, you don't."

"What do you expect? I have two brothers."

"Shall I send Stacy to live with you for a while?"

"No way, no thanks."

Lake Geneva was a resort town just a few miles from the Illinois and Wisconsin border. After the Great Chicago Fire in 1871, many of the city's wealthiest citizens had mansions built around the lake, as permanent homes, or summer escapes. The area became a playground for the famous and not-so-famous. Today, the rich still lived there, but the town was a resort for all, with restaurants, spas, hotels, boats, and quaint little shops.

Josh's great-grandfather had made millions manufacturing beer. He built a mansion on Lake Geneva, which he lost in the Great Depression of the 1930s. The family still had a small cottage on the property they kept. Josh believed it had been the servants' quarters years ago. It was a cute, white-frame, two-bedroom cottage with lace curtains and wooden furnishings. The porch was quaint with two white wicker chairs. When Josh pulled the brass doorknob, it squeaked. Nautical items, such as anchors and paddles, adorned every wall. The kitchen was small with vinyl floors and dark wooden cabinets, but nobody cooked there. A garage was added a few years ago. Any property facing the lake was expensive, and worth keeping up.

Lori had been there with Josh's family. This was the first time they would be alone.

They pulled into the garage, dropped their bags, and walked into town. Lori was starving, so Josh took her to Popeye's, his favorite local restaurant, just a short walk away. They were led to a cute wooden table facing the water on one side and a wall decorated with fishing items on the other side.

Josh pointed to a heavy wooden fishing rod attached to the wall.

"There's one just like it in the cottage. My grandfather loved to fish. He once had a nice size boat."

The waitress, a plump blonde girl, hurriedly threw a menu on the table. A tall, thin busboy with tattoos covering both arms, gave them water, silverware, and a basket of warm rolls.

Lori didn't bother to open the menu.

"I've been dreaming of their Cobb salad. What are you having?"

Josh smiled.

"Fish. It's usually fresh."

After lunch, they walked around town and window shopped. Lori stopped in front of one that featured clothes for teens.

"Josh, isn't that top adorable? I'm going to try it on."

As she opened the door, Josh backed away.

"I'm not going into a girls' place. I'll wait out here."

Lori's tall, blond, muscular guy was a bona fide jock. He always played the masculine card. Star of the school basketball team. Nothing like Lori's dad, who was attuned to the three women he lived with, four if you count Lassie, and not very outgoing with his masculinity.

Lori went inside and quickly decided the top wasn't for her. Josh barely grunted.

In the past, they had walked around the lake on its famous path or had biked through the area. Today, they decided to go back to the cottage. They bought bread, cheese, and snacks in case they decided to stay in for dinner. Lori had half her salad in a take-home box. Josh had finished his perch and beer. Lori thought he was served beer because he looked old enough.

They put the food in the fridge and walked along the beach for a short time. As Lori stopped to adjust her sandals, she grabbed Josh's arm.

"Stop a minute, Josh, and admire the setting sun. Doesn't it look like a big orange ball melting into the lake?"

"I'm beginning to feel like my parents. Admiring setting suns."

To Lori, it felt like Josh had been acting anxious since they got to the cottage. She wondered if he needed something active to do.

"I hear they have a zip line up here now. If you want to try it, I'm willing."

He looked at her with a blank expression.

"A zip line is not what I need. Let's go back to the cottage."

As soon as they stepped inside, Josh pulled Lori to him. His lips embraced hers, while his tongue explored every part of her mouth. Lori pulled away.

"Let's go in the bedroom. I hate standing by the open window."

"We are facing the water, Lori. No one will see us."

Nonetheless, they headed upstairs to the bedroom. By the time they got there, Josh was hard and ready.

In the two years they had been together, the only sex they had was hurried in the back seat of a car. Lori wasn't sure if she was ready for the adult type of sex in a bedroom, but Josh, a healthy teenager, certainly was, without a doubt. She trembled with excitement and fear, but she was going to bed with a man she loved, and who seemed to love her back.

Josh made sure that his and her clothes came off in record time. Within minutes, it was over before Lori realized they hadn't used protection. She quickly took a shower and decided that one time, especially so fast, wouldn't cause any problems.

They finished off the bread, cheese, and leftover salad and made sure everything was turned off and locked up before they headed home. Her long black hair was still damp from the shower, so Josh kept the top up. It was late enough that traffic was light, though they heard sirens blasting in the other direction. Josh dropped off Lori at 11 p.m. Before opening the car door, he pulled her close and moved his hand up her shorts as he kissed her on the lips. She felt a shiver up her spine upon exiting his car. Lori quietly entered her house and pulled the shade back from the kitchen window to watch Josh pull away. She thought about his hungry touch, and his muscular body. She smiled happily, as she tip-toed up the stairs to her bedroom.

Chapter Ten

With every family member busy doing their own thing, Babs decided to visit Tillie, her great aunt. Tillie's daughter, Lizzie, had asked Babs to come over and help plan her mother's 100th birthday party. Reaching that milestone deserved a celebration. Babs called Lizzie before she left, just to make sure they were home, but at the ages of 77 and 99, they never really went anywhere. Skokie was once a suburban Jewish neighborhood. Now it was occupied mainly by people from India, with saris, gold jewelry, and unusual-smelling spices—and still some very Orthodox Jews. In the past, it had been known for its Jewish delis, restaurants, and stores. Now, the stores had either gone out of business, like most of the kosher butchers, or moved to Highland Park or farther north, where younger Jewish families continued to settle.

It was about a half-hour drive north. Aunt Tillie lived in the same three-bedroom bungalow her family had moved to in the early 1970s when they left South Shore. When Lizzie's husband died, she sold her larger, more expensive house in Northbrook and moved in with her mother. It was easier for Tillie to stay put and a better idea financially for them both.

Babs parked in front of the Chicago-style yellow brick bungalow. The four front windows were covered by an orange awning, and the ancient maple tree provided shade on Chicago's sunny days. She stopped to admire the-stained glass picture of birds and flowers on the upper glass of the front door.

She knocked. Before the big crime wave hit all over the city, Aunt Tillie never locked her door. Lizzie, who wore black pants and a flowered top, welcomed Babs with a warm hug.

Her hair is dyed a little too black, almost like an Orthodox sheitel. Tillie wouldn't exactly approve of her daughter wearing a wig like very religious Jews.

Lizzie seemed a bit flustered.

"We are discussing Mom's party. She is coming up with some wacky ideas."

Babs followed her cousin to the kitchen, where she was immediately offered the usual menu of Jewish food.

"Kugel? Brisket? Bagel, and lox?"

"Kugel, please."

No one can leave my great aunt's house without eating.

Babs sat down next to Aunt Tillie. As Lizzie put a plate of kugel in front of Babs, Aunt Tillie walked to the stove and added a few pieces of brisket to her plate.

"You are too thin, Babs. Eat. Eat."

Babs remembered what her mother used to say.

Everyone loves Aunt Tillie. How can you not love someone who always tells you that you are too thin?

The kitchen still had the same dark wood cabinets and maroon-and-blue flowered wallpaper. Instead of blinds, there were white-lace and blue-dotted curtains made by Aunt Tillie years ago. Music from a goldfinch songbird vibrated through the open window, and the black-and-white cat clock ticked loudly. The burners were always loaded with food cooking and aromas wafting through the house. Lizzie made Babs some coffee in an old metal percolator.

Aunt Tillie, dressed in her uniform of a flowered housedress, seemed determined. She pushed her head forward, almost into Lizzie's face.

"Lizzie, I know what I want to do for my one-hundredth birthday. I want to rent a bus, a comfortable one like they use on travel trips, and take the whole family to see our old family building in South Shore. The whole mishpoche from across the country. The youngsters need to know how wonderful it was to grow up in the building with your parents, brothers, sisters, and all their children living right next to you. We used to eat together, play together, and we helped each other in sickness and through whatever troubles we had. That is what we need today. We lived in a village where we knew each other, and everyone helped their neighbors. Yes, there were fights. So, we yelled and screamed. So what? Then, we hugged and kissed and ate, and it was over."

Lizzie wasn't convinced.

"Mom, it wasn't so great. You forgot that when Pa was alive, he was like a dictator. It was a society run by the men. The women had no say so over anything except the children when they were little. And the kitchen, of course. And there was no privacy."

Tillie poured herself a cup of tea and sat down by the red-and-white, chrome-trimmed kitchen table, the one that traveled with her from the family building.

"You were a child and never realized the maneuvering we women did to keep the men believing they were in charge. Today, you women work and still take care of the kinder."

She grinned, then laughed quietly to herself, as if she were savoring a memory.

Babs put down her fork and wiped her face. The kugel was delicious as always. With its mix of noodles, cheese, raisins, and cinnamon. She had tried to make it several times and it never worked. Aunt Tillie wasn't big on explaining the details of her recipes or the exact quantities of each ingredient.

"A bissel of this and a bissel of that."

"A little of each?

"Exactly!"

When Babs once asked her how she made her chicken soup, Aunt Tillie told her to put water up to a certain mark on her soup pot, one that was so old they would never find another one like it.

She looked up to her great aunt, who was stirring sugar cubes into her tea. Still, she wanted to alert Tillie to the harsh realities they were living in.

"I don't think you realize what the world is like now, especially here in Chicago. According to some, South Shore is one of the most dangerous neighborhoods in the whole country. There are robberies and shootings day and night between the gangs that have taken over. Last weekend, thirty people were shot, and five died. How about we make a video with pictures and friends and relatives talking about the way it was?"

"I have to show you something, Babs."

Tillie slowly stood up, pushed her chair in, and walked down the hall to her bedroom.

Babs looked at Lizzie and shook her head.

"Lizzie, that mother of yours is unreal. Almost one hundred and she moves like a sixty-year-old and is as sharp as can be."

"I'm more than twenty years younger than my mom and have all kinds of trouble—arthritis, high blood pressure, GERD, cataracts, bad knees. You name it. I got trouble with it. The only medicine she takes is an aspirin. I take twelve pills a day."

Babs got up.

"I'll be right back. I have to pee."

Lizzie put another tea bag in her cup.

"I pee all the time. Mom never does."

As Babs entered the bathroom, she thought about her father, fifteen years younger than her great aunt and in terrible shape.

He can't walk, and his mind is gone. Funny how he always made fun of Aunt Tillie.

Ronnie had a habit of criticizing Tillie's old-fashioned Jewish ways and her lack of schooling beyond tenth grade. In her time, many of the girls and boys only had two years of high school. For some reason, Babs' father held that against Tillie.

Babs looked inside her purse for lipstick. She lingered in the bathroom, taking in the 1960s shades of pink. She grabbed a tissue out of the ancient pink poodle tissue box and enjoyed the plushness of the baby pink wool rug. As she passed the front room, she smiled at the plastic-covered red, white, and green flowered sofa and matching chair. The green carpet matched the heavy drapes.

Aunt Tillie's house is a walk into the past.

On her way back to the kitchen, Babs stopped to look at the hallway walls full of black-and-white and color photographs. There were a few of her, her brother, and her mother when they were all young, back in the day. None of her father. She recognized her grandfather, who had died of Alzheimer's.

Great. The genes run on both sides.

Lung cancer was only on her mother's side, but both her grandmother and her mother had died from it.

She shivered and rubbed her arms.

"Do you have a sweater, Lizzie? I'm freezing."

Lizzie pulled a green-and-pink handmade knit sweater out of the closet and handed it to her cousin. Babs admired her aunt's artistic talents.

I can't even sew a button on a blouse.

As Aunt Tillie came out of the bedroom, Babs realized some things about her were different. She was thinner in the middle and her shiny white hair with one black strand was not so thick anymore. Then, she called her by her mother's name.

"Sherrie, here is a picture of the family building. Lizzie's son put it on the computer."

The building was still standing, and looked the same as it did 50 years ago. The picture showed a three-story-plus-basement red brick building with a two-three-two front window pattern. The oak tree was almost as big as the building, and the flowers in front were gone.

"They tore down some of the other buildings, but ours is still there. You know, in all those years, I only went back twice. We can go see it. Maybe someone will let us in. We lived on the third floor. You lived on the second, my brother, Izzy, on the first, and Pa lived across the street with my sister, Sarah, and her son, David."

Lizzie corrected her mother.

"Mom, you're talking to Babs, Sherrie's daughter, not Sherrie. She never lived in the family building."

"My dad calls me Sherrie, too, sometimes. Must be the age. I'm just a few years older than forty-eight—the age my mother died."

"Mom, we can't go to South Shore," Lizzie said. "It's too dangerous. We can have your party here or at Max and Benny's."

The doorbell rang. In walked Yale, Tillie's son, and her face lit up. A son for her generation was special, even though it was the daughters who took care of their parents. Lizzie reached up to hug her brother.

"What brings you here today?"

"The aroma of garlic-laden brisket and onion flavored chopped liver."

Yale grinned from ear to ear.

Tillie stood up and stepped quickly to the refrigerator.

When it comes to food, she's as quick as ever.

She took out her metal roasting pan, a dish from the cupboard, and handed Yale a plate of brisket and potatoes.

"I'm sorry, Son. I don't have chopped liver, but I can make some if you have time."

Yale immediately dug into the plate of food, which Lizzie noticed, too.

"Really, Yale. What are you doing in Skokie?"

"Checking out an office building for a client. Jerry sent me."

Yale worked for his third wife's father, who happened to be a big real estate mogul in Chicago. His first wife's father owned a clothing store, and his second wife's father was a suburban police chief. That one almost put him in jail. Babs couldn't remember how many kids and grandkids he had, except there were many scattered across the country.

Babs eyed her mom's first cousin, the one she heard so many stories about—divorces, girlfriends, shady business deals. He loved to tease her when she was little. In his 70s, he was still good-looking, not as thin, but no pot belly either like most older men. He probably had the best hairpiece she had ever seen, and he was always dressed in the latest fashion. She thought the open-necked business shirt under a sports jacket was his trademark. Today, the jacket was bright blue.

I never see anything like it in the Neiman Marcus catalog.

Finally, Yale noticed Babs inspecting him. He held his fork in the air, eyes wide open, and stared back at her.

"Babs, what are you doing here? I loved your mother, my favorite cousin. After what she put up with, she deserved a longer life."

Everyone felt sorry for Babs' mother while she was married. Her husband was a bastard when Babs was growing up. As soon as her mother died, he was nicer to his kids.

My brother doesn't think so, but I do.

Her Great Aunt Tillie took it upon herself to answer Yale.

We Won't Go Back

"They are helping me plan my one-hundredth birthday."

"When will it be? I want to make sure I'm in town."

Tillie rolled up a newspaper and gently hit him on the head.

"You *better* be here. My birthday is August 20. We are thinking of Labor Day."

"Here?"

Lizzie shood her head.

"I think Max and Benny's."

Yale took his empty plate to the sink.

"I know them. I'll take care of the room, the food, and drinks."

Aunt Tillie stuck her hands out.

"Lizzie, you didn't tell him about the bus."

"Mom, that won't work."

Lizzie turned to her cousin.

"She wants to hire a bus to take everyone to see the family building in South Shore."

"You're kidding, right?" Yale said. "I haven't been back there since we moved out in the early seventies."

Yale got up, pushed the chair back in, and kissed his mother.

"Mom, I have to go."

Tillie hung onto him.

"You'll make the bus work. You know people."

"Yeah, Mom, I'll do my best."

Yale walked out the door and into his silver BMW.

Tillie walked toward the bedroom, muttering to herself.

"We should have stayed. It was a beautiful neighborhood right by the lake. The family would have stayed together. Now, they are scattered across the country, and this one doesn't talk to the other one."

She shook her head and tightened her lips as she walked into her bedroom. Lizzie watched her and shrugged as she and Babs watched her disappear.

"It's Mom's nap time. Will you come back and help us plan the invitations and the party?"

"Of course. May I bring my girls? They need to hear some of the family history."

"Mom will be delighted. We haven't seen your family in a long time. Since Mom is so old, we don't go anywhere, especially with Covid. We still wear a mask out."

Babs had switched her phone on off, so as she exited the house, she quickly scanned it. No emergencies, just a message from her girlfriend, Jill, about exercise class and lunch, and one from Shirley about needing her law skills. Babs was a real estate lawyer who hadn't worked during the pandemic because most of her business dried up and she liked being home with her girls. Still, some of her friends still sought her out for legal advice.

As she opened the car door, Lizzie came running out with a package.

"Mom would kill me if I didn't send you home with some brisket and rugalach."

Babs took it and laughed.

Aunt Tillie always sends her love through food.

"Oh my God, I thought this might be the first time I left your house without any food. I was afraid I would have to cook. Thanks."

Babs drove off, thankful for being part of such a loving family.

Chapter Eleven

Babs was munching on a Cobb salad when her phone rang. She shrugged as she looked at Jill, her ultra-thin, perfectly blonde friend and neighbor. They had been discussing their daughters, and how excited Stacy and Lin were about their upcoming school dance.

Babs slowly put down her fork and stared straight ahead. Then, she dropped her cell phone on the floor and covered her mouth with both hands.

Jill was shocked.

"Babs, what's wrong?"

She noticed two strangers at the table next to them look up in alarm. Babs nervously twirled a lock of hair around her fingers.

"What's wrong? Is your friend okay?"

"Can we help? We're nurses."

"My dad died!"

Babs almost yelled. Jill reached across the table and took her hand.

"Oh God, I'm sorry, Babs. I know you expected it, but oh my God. You've been telling me how bad he's getting."

Babs took a deep breath and nodded. Jill squeezed her hand.

"At least he won't be suffering anymore."

"I'm not sure he even knew he was suffering."

She lifted her fork and put it right back on the table.

"I've known for a while that he was in the last stages of Alzheimer's, but right now all I can think of is the father I had *before* that terrible disease. Knowing that he was dying is different than knowing he just died."

Babs gathered her bag and keys and stood up.

Jill, I have to go. There are things I need to do."

"Babs, can I do anything? Take care of the shiva? Pick up Stacy?"

"Thanks, Jill, I don't know. I will let you know."

Babs looked in her purse and pulled out a twenty to cover lunch. Jill gave it back to her. "Forget it, go take care of things."

Babs grabbed her sweater and sunglasses.

Keep moving. You're okay. Keep moving.

When the doorman brought her car around, she wasn't sure where to go first. As she buckled up, she remembered Larry, her father's law partner and friend. He was the source of the money needed to keep the house going, and he had instructed Babs to call him before anyone else when her father died.

First, she tried to call her brother, but there was no answer. She texted.

DAD DIED.

Babs stared at the words, waiting for Jim to respond.

Weird. When I see those words, it almost helps me accept that it's true.

Larry called her back immediately.

"Babs, your father planned everything. I need you and Jim to come to the office right now and meet with the rabbi and me. Good thing it's Friday; We can make the funeral Monday."

Babs twirled a lock of hair in her hand and took a deep breath.

"Larry, I can't drop everything right now and come downtown, and God knows where Jim is."

Larry answered in the same domineering tone her father had always used.

"Babs, you will do what is necessary, just as I will. I expect you and Jim here in an hour."

Her cell phone buzzed as he hung up. A few cars honked, motioning for her to get out of their way. The young doorman knocked on her window to see if she was okay. As Babs looked out the window, she realized that she was blocking the restaurant driveway, so she pulled over and tried to collect her thoughts.

Go downtown. even though I'm in jeans and a casual top.

Babs checked herself in the mirror.

I almost forgot. Stacy needs to be driven to some promotion event.

She called Mark and broke the news. Just as she thought, he was calm and didn't seem surprised at all. He told Babs he would take care of things.

How can he be so calm? But thank God he is.

Charles called, his voice quivering. She could tell he was badly shaken up. He sounded almost relieved when she told him she knew. Babs extended her sympathy and thanks to the man who had cared so tenderly for her father for so long.

"Charles, wait for my call, please, and if you don't mind, close the door to Dad's bedroom. Thank you."

Babs twirled her hair and tried Jim again. No luck. She needed her brother now, even though he was difficult.

I need gas and a bathroom. Now.

She stopped at a filling station before getting on the expressway. Her father's old law firm on North Michigan Avenue had always intimidated her. It was like visiting the President: one had to be on their best behavior, dressed perfectly, politely answering all questions, sitting like a lady, dress down over your knees, legs crossed at the ankles, gloved hands crossed on your lap.

Today, she felt no different than the little girl in her taffeta dress and Mary Jane shoes who used to visit her father. The blonde, paper-thin receptionist in her St. John black knit suit told her to have a seat, that Mr. Eltin would be with her shortly.

Everything about the office suite was luxurious, from its ultra-high ceilings, comfortable white leather-backed chairs, and ceiling-to-floor, ultra-sparkling windows, to the hydroponic water, which was served in a crystal flute instead of in a plastic bottle. She remembered there was a cafeteria with blue ice cream and an employee gym and spa one floor below.

I feel like I'm here to see a queen instead of a lawyer.

Larry Eltin, who had once been the most handsome man in the firm, slim with a full head of curly, sandy-colored hair, was now bald, wrinkled, and fat. He was still dressed in one of those $1,000 suits Babs used to see her father wear, and she noticed a familiar gold and diamond ring on his pinky finger. Once his former partner retired, Eltin became the president of the firm.

I wonder if his cancer has come back. Larry's much too vain to let himself go like this.

He reached over his massive wooden desk to shake her hand.

"Sorry about your dad passing, Babs. It broke my heart to visit him. You know how close we've been for years, ever since law school. That Alzheimer's is a miserable disease."

Babs nodded.

He seems sincere.

"So, where's Jim?"

"Larry, he doesn't talk to me. He seems to be in a world of his own. Besides fighting over Dad, we have different political views. I keep trying him on his cell phone, calling and texting."

"I tried, too, but the number and the e-mail I have no longer work. Jim needs to sign a document, saying that he will go along with the funeral arrangements, and that he won't contest the will. I also need you to sign."

He passed a few papers across the table.

"Sign right here."

"Larry, what is happening with the will?"

"We will read it at the house on Monday after the funeral."

She signed the paper.

"Okay, I'll keep trying Jim. I need to go now."

"Babs, wait. I want to tell you a few things."

She reluctantly sat down in one a plush, designer chair.

"Your father was an important man, Babs. Besides being president of this firm, he worked for the State Department and was a judge and an ambassador."

Do I need to hear more of what I already know?

"He arranged his funeral down to the last item. Everything is paid for, including his casket. The funeral will be held at the Reform Shalom Synagogue, with Rabbi Jeffery Weintraub officiating, on Monday, June 20, and he will be buried next to his parents in the nonsectarian section of Shalom Memorial Park in Palatine. We will have a catered meal at the house afterward. There will be no shiva after Monday. You should let any family and friends know about the arrangements. I will contact his business associates. Your father even wrote his own obituary. Any questions?"

He wrote his own obit? Oh my God, that figures.

"Larry, when did he make these arrangements?"

"Three-and-a-half years ago when he was in the early stages of the disease. He kept it hidden from everyone but me. He traveled to doctors everywhere, but there was no cure. He even took that new cognitive test, hoping to dispute what the doctors were telling him. About two years ago, when Ron entered the middle stage where he lost so much of his short-term memory and had bouts of depression, he moved from the condo to the house and asked me to talk to you. He trusted you, and so do I."

Babs sighed and twirled a strand of hair around her finger.

"I remember that conversation. I was flattered that my father wanted me to be his helper, but it was devastating to hear that he was in the middle stages of Alzheimer's. It feels like he went downhill so fast."

I still can't believe he's gone.

"Ron was wealthy enough to hire people to do things for him, just about anything, so it was relatively easy for him to hide it, at least in the beginning stages. He always had a driver, you know, so when he became unable to drive himself or communicate, I made sure he was covered by all the hired help he needed."

Larry's phone rang. He excused himself for a moment and wrote something down on a pad of paper, which he handed to Babs.

"The rabbi is busy now. Here is a number for you and Jim to call. The rabbi would like to talk to you both before giving his speech about your father."

It was clear to Babs that Larry was finished with her, so she picked up her purse and turned to leave.

"My condolences to you and your family, Babs. I'll see you Monday at ten a.m. Remember, the service will be at eleven at the temple. The internment will be at Shalom. Make sure your girls are dressed appropriately."

Larry stood up, indicating that their time was up.

Just another meeting on his agenda. Okay.

Babs slowly walked out of the office. She had taken care of her father for two years, and now she was being treated like a stranger. Maybe Jim was right. She would contact her friends and her mom's family, but after his sister died, her dad refrained from talking to the rest of his family, so far as she knew.

I just want this to all be over.

The drive home was full of traffic, but she didn't care. Her phone kept beeping. Unfortunately, Jill had told all her friends about Babs' father dying, and they were all reaching out to offer help. Still, Jim hadn't called. He and Babs couldn't stand each other, at least on the surface, but they were still the only kin each other had and Jim was the only one Babs could talk to about her youth and her father.

I don't hate him. I just can't get through to him, and it's so frustrating!

Someone honked. Babs flinched and looked at the speedometer. She was going 45 m.p.h. on the expressway.

I'm driving like Cousin Lizzie.

She sped up. When she finally got home, Babs was happy to find Lassie, who was the only one there. Mark had left a note.

Took the girls to dinner. Available to help with the arrangements.

Babs laughed as she went upstairs, thinking about how her father had already arranged everything. She sat in a lounge chair and stared at a photo of her mother.

If only Mom was alive.

A few minutes later, Stacy came running into the bedroom in her cute blue-jean shorts. "Mom, I got picked to speak at my promotion. Will you help me with my speech?" *Clearly, Mark hasn't told the girls about their grandfather's passing.*

"Yes. Of course."

Stacy pursed her lips, obviously displeased with her mother's lack of enthusiasm.

"You don't even care. I hate you."

As she ran out of the room, Mark caught her.

"Stacy, stop. Listen, your mother's father, your Grandfather Ron, just died. Help her."

"She didn't like him any better than she likes me."

Stacy turned and went to her room. Lori, who heard the conversation, walked over to her mother, and hugged her.

"I'm sorry, Mom. What can we do?"

Babs burst into tears. Her emotions were a tangle of relief and sadness. Tears for the father she had grown up with, for better or for worse, and tears for the fact that she was barely 50 and an orphan. She even shed a tear for having a daughter who temporarily hated her.

Mark gave her a tissue and Lori brought her some water. When Babs settled down, she told them about her visit to the lawyer.

Mark laughed.

"What a character your father was, Babs. Hey, now you don't have to worry about putting the whole funeral together or paying for anything. It's a blessing. All you have to do on Monday is show up."

Stacy reemerged.

"Monday? Do I get to miss a day of school?"

Chapter Twelve

The weekend was a blur, with non-stop phone calls and a flurry of activity, as everyone picked out just the right black outfits to wear as the mourning family. Babs searched through her closet and chose a St. John black knit suit, which would require a foundation garment to hold in her growing stomach.

At least it's a designer outfit.

She refused to buy something new. Her matching black purse and low heels looked like a perfect ensemble for a funeral. Lori wore a plain, dark gray dress, and adorned with Babs' pearls, it would work well. Stacy, not surprisingly, found something to complain about.

"I'm not wearing this stupid outfit you picked out."

They made a quick trip to the mall, where Stacy found a cute white top, a flattering navy skirt, and navy flats. Babs allowed her to add the small diamond studs her grandfather gave her for her Bat Mitzvah.

Mark shook his head when he saw her.

"It's a funeral, not a fashion show!"

Babs shrugged.

"It's a Jewish funeral. You wear your best."

On Saturday night, with still no response from Jim, Babs called Trish, his ex-wife. They were still good friends, and Babs thought Trish would know where her husband might be. They co-raised three boys. Babs wished they would get back together. Trish was only five feet tall, thin, and cute as a button, but she was tough as can be. When she felt the need, she could flare up those Irish green eyes of hers and shout out orders.

"You're kidding!" Trish said. "Is the infamous Ronald Greenspan dead? Sorry, Babs. That just popped out."

"It's okay, Trish."

"I'll find Jim for you. It's his weekend with the boys. Oh, and Babs, don't talk to him about the abortion business. He's all wound up about killing babies. You know, his first wife, Kitty, had an abortion without telling him."

Babs nodded.

"I remember. She was a piece of work. I think he married her to get a rise out of our father. I remember Dad telling him, 'You *use* whores, but you never marry them.' Listen, Trish, please try to find Jim, for his sake, and for your boys. Our father was very wealthy, and he should have left us some money. God, I know you need it. Is Jim working?"

"No, and he is way behind on child support."

Babs heard Lassie barking and sniffing around downstairs, as if she just noticed something different than the usual household sounds and smells. She hung up her phone and ran to the landing to check out the commotion. She perked up when she saw her best friends, Jill, and Julie, come in with a pizza from Lou Malnati's.

Babs grabbed her bathrobe and joined them in the kitchen. They all hugged and found seats around the kitchen table, where they ate and talked. Mark stole a piece of pizza and a beer and went into the den, leaving the girls alone.

"Where are Lori and Stacy?" said Jill. "Don't they want some pizza?"

Babs smiled.

"Stacy is sleeping over at Joanne's house, and Lori is out with Josh."

Julie opened the fridge and took out a Diet Coke.

"Babs, your daughter has the most popular guy in the school wrapped around her finger. He's crazy about her. My Katy is jealous."

"We like Josh, but they both are young and will probably go to different colleges. He has a basketball scholarship to Tulane, and Lori will most likely go to the University of Illinois in Champaign. She would like to follow him to Tulane. She could get in, but out-of-state colleges are up to sixty, seventy thousand dollars a year."

Julie looked up and frowned.

"Tell me about the cost. I have four of them to put through college."

"This is the best damn pizza," Jill said.

She stuffed a big piece into her mouth, dripping with red sauce and cheese.

"Can you believe what is happening now with abortion and gun laws? What does your friend, Shirley, think?"

"Shirley sent me an e-mail. Let me read it to you."

Babs scrolled through her phone.

"It says, 'We are a group of old lawyers who have always worked within the law. We plan to fight the Supreme Court decision by encouraging people to vote for candidates who think as we do, so they can change the laws through Congress and sign petitions for new laws. We will also join rallies and television debates. Enlist your friends to join us.'"

"Good, that they aren't radical." Jill said.

She got up to go to the bathroom.

"I like the way Shirley and her group are approaching this. Count me in to help."

Julie picked up a newspaper on the counter and turned to the obituary.

"You never told us how important your father was, Babs. Besides the obit, the *Tribune* dedicated a whole page to him."

Babs' cell phone rang. When she saw her brother's name, she grabbed it and moved into a private room.

"The bastard finally died," Jim said. "You left me a message about his plans to be honored like someone special. I want no part of it."

"Jim, please. Don't hang up. Think about your kids. Dad was very wealthy, and your family needs the money and I need your support."

"I want nothing from that man."

"Why are you so bitter? Okay, I'm sorry. I know he hit you, but you continued to antagonize him. Mom always tried to protect you from Dad."

"Besides the beatings he gave me, one day I watched him rape our mom."

Jim's voice was steady and emotionless.

"He slapped her. Then, he threw her onto the bed and got on top of her. She was crying, calling out, 'Please stop! You are hurting me.' "

Jim paused and then continued.

"I didn't help her."

Babs twirled her hair in her fingers.

"Jim, Mom always said that Dad abused her emotionally, but never physically. Maybe you are wrong. Maybe they had that kind of sex. Who knows? You were just a kid. You told me something like this before. You need therapy, Jim. Really. I did it, and it helped me understand."

Babs leaned against the wall, overcome by memories. It took her a few minutes to realize Jim had hung up. She tried to call him, but no luck. She called Trish to remind her to get Jim to the funeral because she guessed that her father's required it. If either one of them were to inherit anything at all, they had to be at the reading of the will, which would take place right after the burial.

I don't remember Dad ever physically hurting Mom, but she did hide whenever anything became controversial.

We Won't Go Back

It had taken Babs years of therapy and a kind and loving husband to get the help she needed to deal with her childhood and the world in general. Jim needed therapy, too, especially now, but he wouldn't go near it. He was almost 50 and had been through three marriages and three divorces. He had three kids, and God knows how many jobs he blew because of anger issues. Babs was grateful to Trish, who couldn't live with him, but still loved him and tried to help however she could.

Babs got a text from Larry about Jim. She wasn't sure how to answer.

"What about Jim?"

"I'll let you know as soon as I hear from him."

When she reentered the kitchen, Julie handed her a glass of white wine.

"I thought you might need this after talking to your brother."

Her friends had cleaned up and were ready to go. They knew Babs needed time alone. She hugged them both, walked them to the door, and sat down in the kitchen.

A few minutes later, Lori appeared. She looked pale and had tears in her eyes.

"What is wrong?"

Lori didn't answer. Babs asked the only question she could think of in that moment.

"Did you and Josh break up?"

"No, Mom, we just disagreed."

She ran up the steps to her bedroom without elaborating.

At least he didn't hit her.

Babs finished her wine and slowly walked upstairs. Lori's door was closed, so she ducked into her own bedroom, where Mark was snoring. She brushed her teeth, took her pills, and tried to find a place to sleep somewhere between Lassie and Mark. It was already midnight, and the funeral was tomorrow.

I know I'm not religious, but I feel like I should pray. For something.

Before she could come up with anything, Babs drifted off to sleep.

Chapter Thirteen

Ronald Green Esq. was buried on June 24th, the same day the Supreme Court overturned Roe. It was a sunny bright morning, when the family should have been out playing, or shopping for colorful clothes. Instead, nearly everyone was dressed in somber shades of black and grey, with the occasional dark blue or green. Babs, Mark, Stacy, and Lori were picked up in a luxury limo and driven south on Lake Shore Drive to Shalom Synagogue. Everyone sat quietly, except for Stacy, who examined the limo and asked questions of the driver.

"Do you like driving a limo?"

"Yes, Miss, I do."

"Do you make a lot of money?"

"I do okay, Miss."

"Why do you have all these fancy glasses?"

"If you need a drink, Miss."

"Are you going to serve us drinks?"

"Sorry, no, Miss. But help yourself."

Lori was irate. She glared at her sister.

"Shut up, Stacy. Mom is already nervous enough."

Babs didn't bother to look at her daughters.

Miss? Really? What century is this driver living in?

She twirled a strand of hair in her fingers.

Babs' nerves were shot. She had cried that morning while looking for her mother's diamond heart necklace. She wanted to wear it as a symbol of their bond and as a reminder that she did have one parent who had loved her unconditionally, without imposing their own agenda. She hated that she would soon be the center of attention, especially with strangers.

I could never be a trial lawyer. Or a politician.

Babs had no idea if Jim was coming, and no one else did either.

As the limo pulled off the outer drive, Babs took note of a large Moorish building with colorful stone arches and wooden columns. She had noticed it before, but never knew it was a synagogue. When the limo pulled up to the entrance, Babs and her family wasted no time leaving the limo.

Let's just do this and get it over with and go home.

The inside was even more beautiful than the exterior, with its enormous, luxurious organ and its delicate, carved wooden pews. From looking at the entrance and the large lobby outside the sanctuary, it was hard to tell it was a Jewish synagogue.

This is beyond Reform.

Inside the sanctuary, Babs looked at the bimah, the stage area where the synagogue held their services and where the funeral service would soon begin. Inside the ark were ten Torahs, a large collection, which only a wealthy congregation could afford. In the Jewish religion, a temple's worth was often determined by how many Torahs it owned, not by the value of its physical building.

Even though the obituary asked for donations to several charities, the room was overrun with brown, white, and blue baskets of lilies, daisies, carnations, and roses. The funeral director ushered Babs and her family into a small, private room, where they were could view the body.

Once upon a time, her father was 6'2" and 180 pounds.

Mom was so short she hardly reached his chin.

Babs twirled a strand of hair in her fingers.

Now, the emancipated body in the mahogany casket was unrecognizable. He was dressed in an expensive suit, and someone had done a professional job with his make-up, especially the red blush, but nothing could disguise the white face of death.

Babs looked around the room, searching for Jim. She noticed an odor of perfumed death and felt nauseous. She left the viewing of the casket quickly and collapsed into Mark's arms.

The funeral director entered and stopped short when he saw Babs.

"Did you see my brother?"

Jim wouldn't answer her calls.

Trish had left a message.

"I'm still working on it."

The director shook his head and left the room.

Rabbi Weintraub entered the room and shook everyone's hand. He tore the traditional black mourning ribbons and instructed each member of the family to wear one. Years ago, even secular Jews ripped their clothes to symbolize their loss. But today, only those living in Orthodox communities upheld that custom. Reform and Conservative congregations tore ribbons instead, which was plenty for Babs and her family.

Stacy was fidgeting with her ribbon.

"This thing doesn't match my outfit."

Lori almost hit her.

"It's black, silly. It goes with anything."

"Whatever."

The rabbi looked confused and turned to address the family.

"Do any of you want to speak about your father or grandfather?"

Babs watched Stacy's eyes open wide in terror.

"No! No way!"

"Larry asked to speak," Rabbi Weintraub said. "Is that reasonable with you? He and your father have been valuable members of our congregation or a long time. They donated a large sum of money to our museum. You should visit someday. We have more than five hundred artifacts."

There is so much I don't know about my father.

They were led out of the room and into the sanctuary, where they were seated in the first row, next to the casket. Nearly 200 people were there to honor Babs' father, including judges, lawyers, aldermen, statesmen, and friends. Even more would have come had they been able to catch a flight in time.

Babs didn't recognize most of the people who shook her hand and offered condolences. Masks were optional, and she worried about the new strain of Covid. Babs was relieved when everyone was finally asked to take a seat.

Rabbi Weintraub, with his salt-and-pepper beard, and wearing his white-and-blue tallis, looked the part as he stepped up onto the pulpit and gathered everyone's attention. For the next 40 minutes, he praised Ronald Green, and then Larry spent at least 20 minutes listing the accomplishments of his former partner and friend.

Aunt Tillie was seated behind Babs in a long black dress. She tapped her on the shoulder and tried to whisper, but anyone nearby could hear her.

"I hate it when a live bastard becomes a dead angel."

Hmm. When a bastard in life becomes an angel in death?

"Don't do that to me, Babs. Promise me."

Babs couldn't help but quietly laugh. Her 99-year-old great aunt was still as sharp as could be.

Stacy tugged on her mother's sleeve.

"I think Uncle Jim is in the back row."

Babs turned and saw her brother with Trish and his oldest son, Brian. She sighed in relief, even though she knew that she couldn't count on him for anything. Babs motioned to Jim, but Mark reached in to gently put her hand down.

"Leave him alone for now. He knows you are here, but he doesn't want to be recognized."

The rabbi read from the Psalms and asked everyone to join him in reciting the mourner's Kaddish. Once the casket was wheeled out of the sanctuary, Babs and her family began the recessional, and the guests followed.

As Babs looked in vain for Jim, she and the family were shuffled into the limo for the long ride to the cemetery. Barely 50 people showed up, much to Babs' relief, and the rabbi led a short service with no more speeches. As he recited the Kaddish again, Babs looked for Jim, but he was nowhere to be found. Then, she realized her father had chosen to be buried with his parents instead of next to her mother.

At least they're both here.

Shalom was one of the newer, park-like Jewish cemeteries, located in Arlington Heights, a northern suburb of Chicago. She hated the old cemetery on the West Side where most of her mom's family were buried. It was crowded and not kept up.

Mark and I need to get plots in the non-sectarian section.

She knew that it was up to her to take care of it, that she couldn't depend on her children to do it.

Just as the casket was lowered into the ground, a torrential rain began. Fortunately, they were gathered under a small tent. After fulfilling the Jewish tradition of shoveling dirt over the casket—albeit hastily—Babs and her family ran across the grass to the waiting limo. As Babs was about to enter the car, she stopped cold and pointed. Mark and the girls almost tripped as they stopped to look.

"The man from the picture!" said Babs.

"What picture?" Mark said.

"The one taken at Dad's house."

Mark and the girls looked where she was pointing, but no one was there.

Stacy moaned as she slid into the limo.

"I want to go home. I'm wet, and my feet hurt in these shoes."

Babs shook her head. Stacy had insisted on those pointed slippers.

"We're going to Papa's house first for shiva," said Lori. "You're lucky we're only sitting today, not seven days."

Stacy couldn't believe it.

"Seven days? Who does that? Are you crazy?"

Mark couldn't resist.

"My religion is smarter. We just get drunk and celebrate that the deceased is going to heaven. Come on, Babs, get in the car. You're getting soaked."

She entered the limo reluctantly, still mumbling about the man she had just seen.

"I'm sure the man I noticed at Dad's grave is the same one who's bothering Dorothy."

A Rolls Royce, a Bentley, three limos, and several cars were already parked at the house when they arrived. Babs sat in the limo a moment, reflecting on the day so far.

Why did Dad do this to us? Yes, he spent his whole life trying to be recognized and admired by everyone—except for his family. Jim and I could have used some of the money that always went to charities and the Republican Party. He did put us through college, though. What did he get in return? A non-practicing lawyer and a non-practicing computer expert.

As the family exited the limo, a handful of reporters surrounded them as they headed for the front door. The journalists asked questions and photographers snapped pictures like they were all celebrities. Mark held his cool. He walked his family into the house and made sure no one stopped to answer any questions, especially Stacy.

When they entered the dining room, Lizzie and Aunt Tillie were about to leave. Lizzie hugged Babs.

"Sorry, but we can't stay. This is a party with music and jumbo shrimp on the tables and I need to get my mother out of here. This is a disgrace to our religion."

Babs nodded.

"I understand. I'm sorry. I had no idea what my father chose to do with this whole thing. He never told me anything about his funeral wishes."

Jim, holding a Jack and Coke in his hand, greeted his sister with a big smile. Babs was exasperated with her brother, but glad to see him show up.

I guess he wants the money, after all.

"Dad sure did outdo himself in death. Champagne everywhere so we can celebrate. Go check out the den. There is a video of all his great accomplishments, and a three-piece band is on the patio. Good job, Sis."

He turned his back on Babs and sauntered off. She pushed her way through the crowd until she found Larry.

"What the hell is going on, Larry? This should be a quiet shiva, not a circus with music. Please get everyone out of here."

"Babs, your father planned this down to the last detail. If the party doesn't go on for at least three hours, his will changes. It is one p.m. now. We can clean the house and read the will at four."

People were walking around everywhere holding wine glasses and flutes of champagne. Waiters were making the rounds, holding trays of appetizers, like they do at Bar Mitzvah parties. Someone had already spilled red wine on the white sofa. Dorothy and Charles weren't in sight. Babs could hardly blame them.

"Are you the daughter? Can we get your picture?"

Some newsmen cornered Babs as she tried to step outside on the patio.

"Boy, you Jews know how to do a wake."

Can I just punch this jerk in the face?

Babs grabbed Lori and ran up the stairs. They entered one of the bedrooms, and Babs slammed the door shut. She paced back and forth, crying until her voice became hoarse.

"Lori, tell your father and Jim where I am and what is happening. Nobody can hear a cell phone ring with all that stupid music."

How could I be the daughter of a man with such bad taste?

Mark entered, but he didn't notice his wife's emotional state.

"Stacy and your brother's son are having a great time. Boy, did I misjudge your father."

Mark laughed, oblivious to Babs' anger.

She twisted her hair in her fingers.

"Come downstairs, Babs. The food is great! Jumbo shrimp, lobster, and filet sandwiches. Two senators are looking for you. Maybe you can convince them to reinstate Roe v. Wade."

She glared at him.

How dare you!

"You idiot! How could you say something like that, especially now?"

There was a knock at the door. Larry entered, as if he felt he had a right to barge in without waiting for an invitation. Like Mark, he also ignored how Babs' seemed to be.

"Babs, I'm sorry but we must postpone the reading of the will until next Tuesday. There is someone besides you and Jim who your father wanted at the reading."

Babs was surprised.

"A girlfriend? It doesn't matter. Larry, please tell Jim. Mark, get the girls. I've got to get out of here before I explode."

"I think it's a little late for that, Babs. I'll go round up the girls."

He left the room with Larry. Stacy wanted to stay at the party, but Babs shuffled her family out the back door and they headed home. All she wanted to do was to lie down and put her father out of her mind for the rest of the week. No luck. The local newspaper ran an article the next day about his funeral, and the phone didn't stop ringing. Babs had never really shared her father with her friends. He was there, and then gone from her life and then back full-time. His funeral had made a farce out of their religion.

Dorothy called, wondering what she and Charles should do.

"Would you like us to pack up and leave?"

Babs twisted the hair on the side of her head.

"Dorothy, I don't know what to tell you until the reading of the will next week. Please don't leave. Not yet. We will need you and Charles to help with packing and taking care of things. I will make sure you are paid no matter what happens to the estate."

Besides her house and the girls, Babs had spent a good deal of her time working with Larry and the doctors to provide her father with the proper care, especially over the last year when he entered the third stage of Alzheimer's.

Now that she wasn't caring for her father and his paperwork, she could go back to working with Shirley on an amendment to the constitution to protect reproductive freedom. Shirley and several of her friends had left messages, asking for her help. The Supreme Court had made it official, and it was now up to each state to decide what kind of new abortion legislation they wanted to pass. So far, nine states had passed bills to ban the procedure, and 17 more were expected to do the same. Illinois was expected to continue to allow abortion, which meant the state would need more facilities to accommodate the out-of-state rush, especially from Wisconsin, where abortion was banned.

How sad to think that 50 years ago Shirley and Mom thought they were finally safe.

There was now an abortion pill that wasn't around back then, but it had to be ordered by a physician and used in the first three months. On top of that, it was banned by most states that already banned abortion.

Mark refused to talk to Babs about abortion or her work with Shirley. His upbringing as a Catholic was a real barrier. He always said he wasn't religious, but those early years of his childhood and adolescence had left their mark.

Chapter Fourteen

Stacy's promotion from eighth grade to high school couldn't wait, as much as Babs wished it would. She was proud of her daughter but exhausted from all the commotion of the previous week. Mark's widowed mother would be with them, so Babs knew she had better keep a closed lip. Grandma Mary, a religious Catholic, still couldn't believe her only son had married a Jew. Though after her father's circus funeral, Babs felt it was hard to be proud of her Jewish side.

Stacy was hyped up.

"Mom, where are you? We gotta leave in ten minutes. The seats are first-come, and I want you to hear me give my speech."

Strange to hear Stacy rushing.

Babs finished her makeup, fastened her necklace, and joined the family downstairs.

The promotion was held in the school auditorium. Bright-eyed, smiling kids, 13 and 14 years old, dressed in red satin gowns and matching caps, were laughing, and joking with each other. Each family was lucky to get four tickets, as the auditorium wasn't very big. Extra chairs had been added in every row. The principal reminded the students that they were the first class in two years to not have their promotion online because of Covid. Babs was sorry they hadn't brought masks. Covid was still around, but the new strain was more like a bad flu, so nobody took precautions. Only about ten percent of the crowd wore masks.

Stacy, who loved to talk anyway, did a great job on her speech, though she almost tripped walking up the three steps to the stage. Her family was especially proud when she received an award for educational excellence. According to Stacy, she was always failing. Instead, she received an award for getting straight A's.

Stacy Wood was nearly the last graduate to walk across the stage and collect her diploma from the principal. She always said she would marry someone whose last name started with an A or B, so she could finally be in the front of the line!

The applause thundered through the room as Dina Zumba received the last diploma, and everyone became official high schoolers. That night, they would celebrate at a school dance and Stacy would wear the white lace dress she and her mom had bought weeks ago. Underneath her cap and gown, she wore a comfortable print dress with t-straps.

Outside in the schoolyard, families gathered for pictures, congratulations, and gift-giving. The sun hid behind a group of white fluffy clouds, but the predicted rainfall never arrived.

Thank God. My daughter would've freaked out about her hair.

Stacy had already received a new Apple computer from her parents as a graduation present, a gold necklace from Lori, plus several checks and Amazon cards from other relatives and friends. She moved around to congratulate her fellow graduates. She was so outgoing that she knew everyone's family.

Afterward, she and the family went to a special restaurant in Highwood, called Nite 'N Gale. Stacy and Babs loved their barbecue. Mark and Lori preferred the duck, and Grandma Mary opted for the chicken. Stacy, still excited about her promotion, talked continuously about her upcoming high school year. Lori smiled, enjoying her little sister for a change. Grandma Mary was quiet until dessert arrived. Then, she addressed Babs with a subject she didn't see coming, especially on that day.

"Babs, I hope you aren't getting mixed up in this abortion business."

Are you kidding? Now?

Mark, in a loud authoritative voice, which was not his usual tone, decided to take Babs off the hook and answer his mother directly.

"Mom, we don't talk politics. Especially not now and not here."

"Mark, this isn't politics. It's God's will."

Babs interrupted Mark.

"It's okay. Everyone has a right to their opinion."

She turned to Stacy, hoping to change the subject.

"You looked beautiful on the stage, and afterwards. I love the way the print dress fits you, but Lori and I, and Jill, think Jason was the best-dressed graduate out of all of you. That ruffled white skirt, with his standard cowboy boots and the eye makeup. Oh my gosh."

"Mom, Jason should now be called Janine. She is much better-looking and happier as a girl than as a boy. Please try to call her Janine, and don't make jokes. We all call her Janine and accept her as a girl! Soon, she will be on hormones."

Babs twirled her hair in her fingers.

"I apologize, Stacy. I should not make jokes."

Babs wondered if Janine was also thinking of having surgery. She thought of her mom's first cousin, David, who came out as gay back in the 70s when it was so hard to do.

Different issue, of course, even though they both must be so hard for someone so young.

Grandma Mary shook her head and took a bite of chocolate cake.

"I don't understand any of this."

On the way home, after they let her grandmother off, Stacy approached Babs.

"Mom, Is Grandma Mary wrong about abortion?"

Babs stopped to think before answering. The lawyer in her emerged in how she replied.

"Stacy, she may be wrong according to our thinking because we view it as a rights issue. Our position is every woman has the right to decide what she can do with her own body."

"Mom. Duh."

"To be fair, Stacy, Grandma Mary looks at it from a religious viewpoint. She believes the unborn are persons in the sight of God from the time of conception, and that abortion is murder."

Stacy flinched.

"Judaism says that the life and health of the mother come first, before the fetus."

"That's like common sense, right?"

"Yes, you make a good point, Stacy. You know, I believe the problem in our country is that people no longer try to understand each other or tolerate each other's beliefs. The whole situation scares me. Nobody is one hundred percent right."

"But Mom, you always say the right to choose is yours! Not God's!"

Babs nodded and squeezed Stacy's hand.

Maybe she's been listening, after all.

For the next few minutes, no one talked until they reached home, and Lassie jumped all over them. When Babs and Mark reached their bedroom, he pulled her close to him.

"Thanks for not making my mother the bad guy."

She sighed with relief after removing her bra.

"Mark, I steered the conversation away from that so the girls wouldn't judge your mother, but I do believe what I said."

"You're good, Babs. You need to go back to practicing law, but not now. Tonight, I have another idea."

He pulled her close to him, fondling her naked breasts, while he took her face in his hands and kissed her tenderly. He knew how to please and relax her.

We Won't Go Back

"I love you, and I'm sorry I've been neglecting . . ."
She never got to finish her sentence.

Chapter Fifteen

As Babs stood by the window and watched Kars4Kids take away her beloved 22-year-old car, she felt a tear on her cheek. She had driven that car when she and Jim got married. It had all the modern gadgets, like a tushy warmer.

My perfect golden Chevy.

After the car disappeared from her sight, Babs refilled her coffee cup and joined Mark at the breakfast table.

I'll miss that car, and our family will miss having three.

As she toasted a plain bagel, Lori came running down the stairs, yelling like the world was coming to an end.

"They took my car! I have a summer job at camp. How will I get there?"

Mark looked up from his newspaper.

"Lori, it died beyond repair, and I'm not buying a car you will only use for a year and then go away to college. Work it out with Mom."

His voice did not have its usual soothing tone. Babs noticed and tried to soothe her husband.

"Mark, the girls and I will take care of it."

She was secretly hoping the reading of her father's will would help. Otherwise, she was going to be a chauffeur for two girls all year. Mark thought she should go back to work. They could use the income. She was procrastinating on that issue. Since the time both girls started school, she had worked as a real estate lawyer—until the market dried up from the pandemic. Now, houses were selling again, but Babs preferred volunteering part-time with Shirley on current issues and spending more time with her girls.

She remembered her mother's last speech on the day when more than 200 women gathered to honor her. At the time, they all thought she was retiring young. They didn't find out until later that it was lung cancer, which had made her retire.

"We have been working diligently to not take jobs away from men but to get them to be equal partners in the workplace, and at home."

I'll always remember those words.

Babs sipped her coffee.

I don't think Mom and her friends knew they were setting women up to do everything: work outside the home and take care of the kids and the house.

The pandemic had allowed Babs to stay home and cook and spend time with her girls. Besides her mom's family's lessons in Jewish cooking, she experimented with French and Italian cuisine. Lasagna and creme brûlée became her specialties, although Mark was still a better cook.

He gave her a peck on the cheek and scratched Lassie on the head before he left for work.

"Mom, get up, I have to leave."

Lori shook her mother out of her daydream. Babs took another sip of coffee, grabbed her purse and keys, and followed her daughter out to the car. In her haste, she tripped over Stacy's shoes and let out a swear word. It reminded her to leave a message for her sleeping princess of a daughter, to tell her why she had woken up to an empty house.

After Babs dropped off Lori, she turned on the radio. Murder. Robberies. Rallies. Protests. Gun control. Abortion. Ukraine. Inflation. Stock market.

Isn't there any good news in the world?

She quickly changed the channel to music from the 60s and 70s. She turned up the sound and sang along with the Beatles' *Yellow Submarine.*

Her cell rang. It was Jill.

"Can you meet me for lunch at Walker Brothers? Afterward, we can go to Eileen Fisher's dress shop. They're having a big sale."

"I'll call you back. Stacy is home alone. I need to see if she needs anything."

"Babs, I just dropped Stacy and Lin off at Northbrook Court. They're going to see the new Tom Cruise movie.

Damn it. Lori tells me everything, and Stacy nothing.

"I'll meet you in fifteen minutes. Thanks for taking care of Stacy."

Central Street in Highland Park wasn't as crowded as usual. Babs found a parking space across from Walker Brothers breakfast restaurant and breathed in the sweet cinnamon aroma as she entered. Jill, with her long brown hair and perfect thin body, was sitting in a red leather cushioned booth, just to the right of the entrance. Babs ordered her usual: blueberry pancakes and black coffee, while Jill ordered her usual: eggs. Babs loved their famous apple cinnamon pancake, but that was too much. She and Jill always met in Highland Park. It was such a friendly town compared to where she lived, and they had gift shops, grocery shops, theater, and dress shops, besides their many good restaurants.

As soon as the waiter left, Jill leaned in.

"I've been waiting all week for a call from you about your father's will. If you don't want to tell me, I'll just have to suffer with anxiety."

Babs shook her head and laughed.

"I'm sorry I didn't call you. The reading didn't happen after the funeral. It was postponed until next Tuesday."

Jill smiled.

"That sounds so much like your father. He's creating tumult from the grave."

"By the way, when did Stacy and Lin make arrangements to go to the mall?"

"This morning. Stacy called Lin and cried that she was abandoned by her family, so I picked her up and took them both to the mall."

"My dramatic princess. I left her a message that I was driving Lori to her job. We finally had to get rid of my old car, so I'm going to be a chauffeur this summer."

Their food came. They ate slowly while talking about their friends' problems and what to do with their teenagers. They finished, split the check, and walked across the street to the dress shop. The cool spring breeze was all the encouraged Babs needed to buy a tan, cable-knit sweater, and a pair of matching leggings. She had gained some weight during the pandemic and felt that nothing looked good on her. Jill just never gained an ounce, and her hair was still without one gray hair.

A girl's gotta do what she's gotta do.

They said their goodbyes, and Babs left for Sunset Foods, while Jill picked up the girls at the mall. By the time Babs arrived home and unloaded the groceries, it was almost time to pick up Lori.

Lassie was in front of the patio doors, jumping, and barking away. Babs opened the door and watched her dog leap outside after a black-and-white cat that was stalking the bird feeder. She walked out and stopped a minute to admire her husband's beautiful garden. Trimmed green bushes, a clear blue fishpond, sweet fragrances of the lilies and stargazers, and her favorite, the purple clematis climbing up the fence. Sparrows were splashing in the bird bath, while gold finches sang their hearts out.

I need to sit on a lounger with a glass of chocolate wine in one hand and a book in the other and enjoy my yard.

Her phone beeped with messages. She had to get Lori.

Another day lost in the garden. A third car would be nice.

She pulled in with Lori a few minutes before Jill dropped off Stacy.

"Okay girls, Dad will be home in thirty minutes. I need help getting dinner together. I'll do the salmon on the grill; Stacy, set the table, please, and Lori, please make the salad. There is a Bundt cake in the fridge, and some Sunset double-baked potatoes that need warming. I promised Dad a homemade dinner that he didn't have to make."

Stacy huffed and puffed and headed into the kitchen. Lori drifted off, eyes on her phone.

"Lori, tell whoever you are talking to that you'll call them back."

Lori was outside the patio door by then.

"Josh, I have to go. I'll check with my mother."

She paused a second.

"You better bring protection."

Lori joined her mother and sister back in the kitchen.

"Mom, may I go to Lake Geneva with Josh this weekend?"

"Oh, I wanted to have Aunt Tillie and Lizzie over, but that's okay. Never mind. You can go. I can have them over in two weeks. Josh's family is very nice to invite you to their cottage."

Lori didn't mention that his parents would be at a wedding out of town.

Babs smiled. She trusted her older daughter.

Chapter Sixteen

As Babs opened the drapes to watch the electric flashes of lightning, she heard the rumble of thunder and sat on the bedroom floor, mesmerized by nature's show. She felt Mark's hand touch her back.

"Babs what are you doing? It's three in the morning."

She turned and smiled at her husband.

"Watching Dad's pre-show before the reading of the will tomorrow."

He helped her get up.

"Do you think it will be a circus like the funeral?"

"Yes, I do."

She let him guide her back into bed. She felt safe in his arms. Mark was nothing like her father, who constantly cheated on her mother, and always expected to be in charge. Mark was always there for Babs, and she doubted that he ever looked at another woman. He was a fixer-upper, while her father was a call for help.

Dad was a narcissist.

She drifted in and out of sleep as these thoughts spiraled through her mind all night. When the alarm went off a few hours later, Babs struggled to get out of bed. She dressed in a navy blue and white suit, with low white heels. She applied some make-up base, blush, and pink lipstick, but no eye makeup. She didn't want to eat anything, but she had a cup of coffee.

By eight a.m., she was on her way out the door, headed to the anticipated reading of the will. She kissed Mark and grabbed her car keys.

"Thanks for taking the day off. Lori needs a ride to work and back home. Stacy has a dentist appointment at eleven, and don't forget Lassie."

"Honey, you sound like you will be gone for a week. Calm down. Your father is dead. He can't hurt you anymore."

Mark didn't know Dad that well.

Traveling downtown was slow because of several flooded sections of the road caused by last night's thunderstorms. Mark thought $5 a gallon for gas would keep people off the road, but he was wrong. Traffic was terrible. Babs barely made it to Larry's office by 9:30, the appointed time that Larry had insisted she make on time.

When she passed Trish sitting in the waiting room, she let out a sigh of relief. It meant Jim was there. She followed the receptionist to Larry's office.

The two of them already looked busy. While she had dressed up, Jim was in a t-shirt and blue jeans, always playing the rebel.

"Babs, I was just telling Jim that your father left money for both of you, but it is attached to rules, and one of them is that you watch a video in separate rooms."

Jim jumped up.

"I'm out of here."

Babs grabbed his arm.

"Jim, play Dad's game one last time for your boys. He always came through with the prize if you played the way he wanted. Remember the waterbed. You almost died holding your breath in the ocean so he would buy you anything you wanted."

Jim stared at his sister. Babs twirled her hair in her fingers. Larry stepped forward.

"You both are going to watch a half-hour video in separate rooms."

Larry wiped sweat from his brow as Jim and Babs nodded. She felt sorry for him. Her father had always used Larry for his dirty work.

Jim was quiet, almost like a prisoner resolved to his fate. They were led to separate rooms where a television was set up. Cakes, cookies, coffee, and water were on a small table. A large, maroon leather chair faced the screen. Babs noticed a wall of bookshelves with heavy law books. Then, the lights went out, and she took her seat.

When the video began, Babs nearly fell out of her seat. Her father, in his booming, commanding voice, stood tall and slim, with a full head of black hair. He focused his attention directly into the camera as he told Babs his life story, one she had heard many times before. His father was Jewish; his mother was not; he had a sister; he became a lawyer and rose high in the Republican Party hierarchy as a judge and ambassador. He explained briefly how he had made a lot of money and was leaving 40 percent of it to the temple, his law school, his law firm, a dozen different charities, and a few people, like Dorothy and Charles, two women from his office, and Larry. Babs sat there numb until he said the bulk of his money would go to his children if they obeyed his rules. She was surprised that no girlfriends were mentioned.

I guess they went south when Dad became sick.

Babs smiled.

Dad needs to be in control, even from the grave.

She twirled her hair in her fingers.

Rules, rules, rules.

The video continued.

"Each of my children will inherit approximately twenty-five million dollars. This money will be distributed for ten years, starting the following year on the anniversary of the day I died. This money will be distributed if and only if the Green, Greenspan name has not been shamed in any way by my children or their children. A man's good name is the best thing he leaves for his family. My trusted friend, Larry Elton, and the Greenspan/ Eltin law firm will carry out my instructions, which will be given to you in written form."

He turned around and walked down a grey path until he was out of sight. The lights went on. Babs sat mesmerized. She couldn't move or stop staring at the empty screen, even when Larry entered the room.

"Babs, we are meeting in the conference room."

He helped her get up.

Jim, stone-faced, followed her and Larry. She made it halfway into the room when she stopped cold, shaking and pointing.

"That man! That man is the one who was stalking Dad's house. Get him out of here!"

Jim grabbed the tall, thin, sandy-haired man standing near Larry's desk.

"Who are you, and what have you done to my sister?"

The man pulled away from Jim and straightened his clothes. His voice was strong and confident, not unlike someone else they all knew.

"I am Byron Green, your half-brother."

Jim stepped back and aimed his fist right into Byron's right cheek.

Chapter Seventeen

Babs was tired and wanted to show her daughters another side of the family, so she took them to see Aunt Tillie.

"We need to concentrate on my normal family and help plan Aunt Tillie's birthday party. She's going to be a hundred!"

As soon as they walked in the door, Aunt Tillie embraced the girls and Lizzie grabbed Babs, happy to see her smiling after the heaviness of the funeral.

"We are making cookies," Aunt Tillie said.

"I hope they're chocolate chip," Stacy said.

She hugged Aunt Tillie, who stepped back and stared.

"I don't make easy goyish cookies. Today, you are going to learn how to work with dough. We are making rugelach."

She opened a drawer and pulled out an apron for each girl.

"To keep you clean."

Lizzie held two coffee cups and motioned Babs to follow. They entered the rarely used front room and sat down on the plastic-covered, red-and-white flowered sofa. She turned on one of the Meissen porcelain antique lamps that sat on a mahogany, lion-pawed, carved end table.

Lizzie settled in and turned toward Babs,

"I don't know what your girls know, so I thought this would be a better place to talk. Tell me what happened. Yale's sister-in-law's daughter works at the law firm."

Babs laughed.

The old Jewish pipeline comes through again. We tend to forget about it now, but the kosher grapevine knows everything! Is it worth saying don't repeat what I'm telling you? Lizzie probably knows more than I do.

Babs took a drink of the hot coffee and tried to get comfortable, but the scratchy plastic was annoying.

Lizzie can't remove it until the sofa goes to Goodwill.

The living room was usually empty. In Aunt Tillie's house, family and company gathered in the kitchen. The living room still looked like it did in the 50s, with plastic covered furniture, bright green colored wallpaper, window blinds with white lace curtains, a collection of knickknacks and antique lamps, family pictures on every shelf and wall, and two copper Sabbath candlesticks and a Havdalah candle.

Babs took it all in and turned to Lizzie.

"Okay, here's what happened. First, Dad left money to every place that will honor him: the temple, the law school, his law firm, Israel, the Jewish United Fund, Chicago's museums, where he was on the board of directors, and who knows where else. He left money to just a few individuals: Charles and Dorothy, of course, two secretaries, and Jim and me. Nothing for his grandchildren. The will comes with all kinds of rules, his personal preferences, and Internal Revenue Service regulations. It could be a long time before we see any money."

"Your father always had rules, Babs. Did you ever find the dating agreement he made your mother sign when they were single? He was a lawyer through and through."

"You're right about that. I will look through a box of items that belonged to her.

Babs twisted her hair through her fingers.

"Lizzie, I miss her so much, her smooth voice and the way she calmed everyone down when there was a tragedy or disappointment. I wish I could hear her now, especially with the mishegoss Dad created."

Lizzie nodded and smiled.

"I miss her, too. She was my best friend."

Both women sipped their coffee.

"Okay, Babs, you're leaving out the juicy parts. Who did Jim punch?"

"Lizzie, do you have any wine?"

"Just Mogen David."

Babs laughed.

"Forget it. Prayer wine won't help."

Babs inhaled the pungent smell of cinnamon and raisins cooking in the kitchen.

This is what I'll always remember from Aunt Tillie, the wonderful aromas coming from her kitchen.

She took a deep breath and continued.

"At the reading of the will, Jim and I found out that we have a thirty-year-old half-brother who lives in London. The funny part is, he knew about us, but we had no clue about him. Lizzie, I still don't believe it."

"Oh my God, what a surprise!"

Lizzie put her hands to her mouth.

"Ronnie had girlfriends when he was married to your mother. Do you know the identity of this man's mother?"

"She was the housekeeper in Dad's London townhouse. When we went with him to London one time, he had to move out and stay with a relative, while the woman took care of us. I remember her—she was very nice, and pretty, too. Her long blonde hair didn't match the hairstyle of most London women. I think she was older than our mother. Most of all, I remember her laughing at Dad's rules, and she let us have ice cream for breakfast with those creamy biscuits. I forgot their family name. She played with us and took us places while Dad worked. Her name was Sophia, and she wasn't afraid of him like Mom."

Babs twirled her hair through her fingers and looked at Lizzie.

"Byron. That's his name. My half-brother. He said his dad was fifty and his mother was forty-five when he was born. Even though the baby was a mistake, Dad agreed to a DNA test. When it proved positive, he acknowledged Byron as his son. I don't know if that surprises me or not. Byron brought documentation. Dad's will says he is leaving a set amount of money to his children, but it doesn't name us, or Byron. Who knows? Maybe a dozen more will come forward. It seems so complicated, and it will hold up distribution of the assets."

"Gee, the name Sophia rings a bell. What about Jim?"

Babs shook her head and laughed.

Stacy yelled from the kitchen.

"The cookies are done. Come and get them!"

Babs didn't like telling anyone that Jim punched Byron and put him in the hospital.

Thank God his jaw wasn't broken. Or Jim's hand.

After a night in the hospital to make sure he didn't have a concussion, Byron went back to London without talking to Babs or Larry, who were tearing their hair out over the situation. Larry asserted that he knew about Sophia, but that Ronnie never told him about Byron. He explained that he had rescheduled the reading of the will because Byron had approached him at the funeral with proof that Ronnie was his father. Within days, when Byron launched a lawsuit against Jim, Larry forced Jim to enroll in a four-week anger management seminar.

Aunt Tillie had her own agenda.

"Let's get some plates and forks from the cupboard."

Stacy took four plates and put pieces of rugelach on each one.

Aunt Tillie smacked her forehead with both hands.

"No! Take the pastry off the plates!"

Stacy was confused.

"They are made with butter and the plates are fleishig."

Lizzie tried to calm things down.

"Mom, you should have told her. No harm done, Stacy."

Stacy had no idea about what she had done.

"What is fleishig?"

"Honey, Aunt Tillie keeps kosher. She uses different dishes for meat and milk products. Fleishig means meat, so since the rugelach is made with butter, which is a milk product, you can't put them on plates that are designated for serving meat products."

Stacy rolled her eyes, but she loved her great aunt, so she kept her mouth shut. Tillie wasn't satisfied and she let Babs know about it.

"Why don't your children know what kosher is? They don't have to keep kosher homes, but they should know about that part of our culture. Stacy had a Bat Mitzvah. What do they teach kids at these modern temples?"

Lizzie put the plates in their proper cupboard and changed the subject.

"Mom, Lori would like to make a video for your party. Take out your pictures and start talking about them."

Lori set her phone to record while Aunt Tillie opened a drawer and took out a large bag of photos that she dropped on the table.

"Aunt Tillie, look into my camera and tell us about how you grew up."

"You are taking my picture? Hold on a minute. I need to comb my hair and put on some lipstick."

Aunt Tillie stood up and quickly disappeared into the bedroom.

When Aunt Tillie came back, her face was brighter from some rouge and her wedding rings were on her fingers. She was still in her flower-printed house dress, but the apron was gone, and her shining silver hair was patted down into waves. Babs put on her blue reading glasses to look at the pictures, and Lizzie took out a pair of cheaters. At the age of 99, Aunt Tillie didn't need any glasses at all.

Stacy chewed on another rugalach and looked at her phone while Lori asked questions. Aunt Tillie was happy to "educate" the youngest members of her family.

"Okay Lori, I'll tell you about your family. You can be the one to carry on our history. Your great-great-grandfather and great-great-grandmother came to America from Poland in 1910. They had six kids The oldest was your great grandfather, Jake, who was born in Warsaw. The rest of us were born in Chicago."

Tillie sifted through the pile of old photographs.

"Lizzie, give me the picture of all of us. Thank you. Barbra was the baby. She is missing in this picture because she wasn't born yet. Funny, the boys had short pants, and the girls were covered in dresses from head to toe. I loved that embroidered dress my mother made for me."

She pointed to a long dress with embroidered flowers along the bottom.

"My mother was an expert seamstress. She made extra money by sewing for the wealthy families in the area. Pa was small, but strong. He worked in construction."

The picture was in different shades of black and on a thin copper type of material. They were called daguerreotypes. The girls were fascinated, and Aunt Tillie took notice.

"After my party, you can have the pictures."

Babs was enjoying how much her daughters appreciated the presentation.

Aunt Tillie could do this all day.

"I was born on August 20, 1922, almost a hundred years ago. We were poor. We lived on the West Side of Chicago in a two-bedroom flat with one bathroom for all of us. The best time was when Pa bought two buildings in South Shore. He had made some money in real estate and the stock market. He was smart besides being a hard worker. The family building was great. We all looked out for each other."

She picked up some pictures of family dinners, where more than 20 people were stuffed into small apartments. A flood of memories swept over her, of sweet and sour aromas, boiling chicken soup and homemade bread, and voices shouting to be heard. She recounted how she became the matriarch of the family after her mother died.

"I ran things at that point, especially when all the boys went off to World War II. I guess you could say that I was the only one who would talk back to Pa, not disrespectfully, of course, but in a reasonable voice when I had to explain things to him."

The sharp, piercing whistle of the tea kettle distracted Aunt Tillie. She went over to the stove and poured water from the kettle into one of her delicate, flower-patterned cups. She dipped the tea bag three times before she added a little milk and sugar. Then, she sat down near the table, slowly sipping the hot tea.

Lizzie picked up a picture and showed it to her mother.

"Mom, who is this?"

Stacy leaned in to check it out.

"He's good-looking. Look at those muscles, and the cute smile."

Aunt Tillie glanced at the photograph.

"Oh, that's Danny, my sister Sarah's husband. Out of the three boys who went to war, he never came back. He died in Okinawa, but he left Sarah with a son he never met. I miss my sister. We were so close."

She wrapped her two fingers together and smiled at Stacy.

"Aunt Tillie, why didn't Danny protest and hide in Canada? In school, we read about the Vietnam protestors."

Tillie smiled and shrugged.

"Nobody protested during World War II. The boys were proud to defend our country. The women and children stayed home together in the family buildings. You had to read about the war, Stacy, and the Holocaust, of course."

"The one about the Jews being killed? We read about it in school, and we've gone to the Holocaust Museum here in Skokie. Have you been there?"

"Of course I have, my dear. Many of my friends lost family they knew in the Holocaust. We lost family we never met because most of our relatives came to America in 1900. You know, I volunteered there when it first opened, but I'm too old now."

She turned toward her daughter.

"Lizzie, we should have never left the building. We lived in our own village. We had everything we needed, and we took care of each other. It is lonely here now. Today, nobody knows their neighbor, and I don't think they even want to anymore."

Lizzie nodded.

"You know, we didn't know about abortion or birth control back then. Just abstention, which worked if you were regular. We had many children, you know, but they didn't all live. I lost my oldest to polio. She wasn't even eating real food yet. She was still nursing when she became sick. And by then, it was too late."

Tillie sipped her tea.

"We had no crime back in those days because we disciplined each other's children. Guns were for cowboys and policemen. I don't understand people today."

Aunt Tillie paused before continuing.

"Nobody is left. All my sisters and brothers are gone, and the children are scattered. Do you think anyone will come to my party? Dora and my brother Izzy's kids and grandchildren are in Florida and New

York; your son Billie and his wife are living in Taiwan of all places. Will your sister come with all her grandchildren from the West Coast? I want my family to know each other. Nobody stays together anymore."

She stopped talking and moved her eyes over the scattered pictures. "We'll finish another day. I'm tired."

Aunt Tillie walked slowly to her bedroom. Babs watched her shut the door and picked up another delicious rugelach.

Thank God for family.

Chapter Eighteen

They stayed with Lizzie a while longer, looking at the photographs. Babs was impressed, yet again, with her great aunt.

"Lizzie, I'm having a hard time believing your mother is going to be a hundred. She's sharp as a tack, and she still moves like a younger woman without any help."

Babs picked up a picture of a scrawny yellow cat next to a full-bodied Black woman.

"I never knew about a cat as a pet. The family always had dogs."

Lizzie laughed.

"Remember Etta? That was her cat. She brought him with her when she cleaned our houses. The cat and Pa would fight."

Babs shrugged.

"She was before my time. So was the family building. My mother talked about it all the time. She loved growing up there. Didn't you have a dog that stole food, like one time he took a brisket off the table and ran away with it?"

"That was our dog, Prince. He drove my mother crazy. He stole food from every place, barked continuously, and always had accidents. I think that was why my dad loved him. He never talked back to my mother. I think he was afraid of her."

"Aunt Lizzie," said Lori. "Were there any scandals in the family?"

Lizzie nodded and then picked up two pictures. "My brother, Yale, always got into trouble, like fighting in school, or car accidents, or dating too many girls at once and getting caught. There were two real *scandals* in my lifetime, maybe three. But you must understand that what was deemed terrible in the forties and fifties is now thought of as nothing. So, that's why we must consider history when we judge things from the past."

Stacy picked up a photo of a teenager in baggy shorts with curly, sandy-colored hair.

"This was my mother's younger sister, Barbra. In the forties, she had sex with a boy who wasn't Jewish. Our grandfather, the one we called Pa, was very religious. He went into a rage and banned her from the house and made the family sit shiva as if she had died."

"Like *Fiddler On The Roof*," Stacy said.

"Exactly," said Lizzie. "She went to California with the boy, but they never married. She ended up getting married three times to wealthy men. Pa wouldn't allow us to have contact with her and we lost contact with her. There was no internet, no e-mail, or texting, just letters or stationary phones."

Babs shook her head.

"All the stories about the family start with how wonderful it was to live together, but they all end with everyone having to follow Pa's rules."

"You're right, Babs," said Lizzie.

She took another sip of her tea.

"It was a different time, when it was expected that the oldest male ruled the roost, and the others followed, especially the women."

As Lizzie picked up another picture, tears came to her eyes. Lori and Stacy looked at the photo of a gorgeous, tall, muscular, black-haired, dimpled young man.

"I'm sure you have heard about Cousin David and his struggles with being gay and dying from AIDS."

Stacy picked up the picture to get a closer look.

"Was he the one who met President Reagan, and the actress who loved collies?"

Lizzie nodded.

"That was when being gay was more accepted. When David first knew he was gay, it wasn't at all, and he struggled to keep it a secret. Sherrie helped him come out, and she was there for him when he died."

Lori watched Lizzie as she reminisced about days with her cousins in the family building.

"Being gay today is not a big deal for most people. Kids are even changing their gender."

She glanced through the pictures.

"Some of these are so old."

She picked up a black-and-white piece of cardboard.

"Lizzie, do you know who this is?"

"I think it's family in Poland."

"When Aunt Tillie feels better and can identify everyone, I can make a super video."

"Can I have another rugelach?" said Stacy.

"Mom will want you to take some home."

Lizzie put the tray of pastries in some Tupperware and handed it to Stacy.

Babs laughed.

"I guess I don't have to worry about dinner."

Lizzie handed her a container with roast chicken and kishka.

Stacy took a sniff.

"What's that?"

Babs laughed.

"Kishka. It's made with stuffed beef casing with flour, seasoning, and schmaltz."

"Schmaltz?"

Stacy turned up her nose.

"Chicken fat."

"Yuck."

Lizzie laughed and whispered to Babs.

"Did you ever tell the girls about your Grandmother Bess?"

"Not everything. Just that she wasn't Jewish."

"They should know, but it's up to you, especially now that abortion is in the news all the time. I thought of her when that ten-year-old girl had to go to another state for an abortion."

Babs turned back to the table and shuffled through the pictures. As she picked one up, a big smile crossed her face.

Gary was our lifesaver after Mom and Dad's divorce. He helped raise Jim and me. I would love to find him. I wonder why he disappeared after Mom died. We kept hoping he and Mom would get married. Ronnie hated him. He probably threatened Gary.

Lori looked at the photo.

"Except for the mustache, he looks a little like Dad."

She's right. They're similar in looks and behavior. Gentle. Easy going. And, just like Gary, Mark likes to bike and garden.

"Mom, can we go?" Lori said. "I have work early in the morning. I'll come back and do the video when Aunt Tillie feels better. It's neat having an aunt who is almost one hundred."

Babs stopped in the doorway and turned to her cousin.

"Lizzie, I almost forgot. Larry, Dad's old partner and friend, gave us tickets to see *Jesus Christ Superstar* next Sunday. Mark will be at a conference. Can you join us? We need someone who was around back in the sixties and seventies."

"Thanks, but I can't leave Mom."

"I'll get Yale to watch her. He owes you. Does he help at all?"

"Babs, he's the boy. In Mom's eyes, he can do no wrong. He does help financially. I'll get my granddaughter, Lily, to stay with Mom that day. She is so good with older people. Right now, she's helping us with party decorations."

"Why don't I know her?"

"My daughter, her kids, and grandkids live in California. Lily, who is twenty-one, flew in early for mom's birthday. Mom is right. We really need to get the family together. Don't tell her this, but Bella insisted that she and my son, Billie, come in for the party. I haven't seen them in almost two years. Everyone is so busy and independent now."

Lori was full of questions on the way home.

"Aunt Tillie was without a husband for like forty years. Why? She was attractive in the pictures that show her out of her housedress. Even now, she's thin with beautiful, shiny white hair, and her skin doesn't have those brown, old age spots like Aunt Lizzie and Papa."

Babs laughed.

"If you asked her, she would say, 'These old men are looking for a nurse or a purse, and I'm not giving either.' She loved being the head of the family, but as she became older, so many family members died or moved away. If she was born at a different time or in a less religious family, Aunt Tillie would have been marching right along with us."

Chapter Nineteen

Jesus Christ Superstar, a musical by Andrew Lloyd Webber and Tim Rice, created a lot of controversy when it debuted on Broadway in 1970. The music was well-received, but the depiction of Judas' betrayal of Jesus, along with vivid suggestions of violence and sex, was seen by some as religious blasphemy. It wasn't as controversial as *Hair,* with its nudity and hard stance against the Vietnam War, but the show raised a lot of hackles in American society.

Babs had seen it in college but didn't realize that Lizzie had never seen it. Aunt Tillie and the family were too religious back then to see a show like that.

Babs and the girls planned to meet Lizzie at the Cadillac Palace Theater. They seldom took the train, so it was an adventure for the girls leave from Lake Forest and head to Union Station in downtown Chicago. Thunderstorms had been predicted for later in the day, which is why Babs decided not to drive. Her head was pounding from the humidity since she suffered from sinus and tension headaches.

All three of them dressed up for the occasion. Stacy wore a cute, brown-and-yellow swinging cotton dress, Babs chose a black dress with silver jewelry, and Lori selected black tights with and an oversized black and white top.

They sat down on worn red vinyl seats, facing each other, for the nearly one-hour trip. The train was nearly empty, probably because of the weather and the fact that the Cubs were not in town, playing a day game, which always meant the city was jammed.

Babs hoped to enjoy some good conversations with her daughters on the ride, but as soon as the train departed, they were glued to their phones. Lori looked up every once in a while to answer a question, but Stacy never even pretended to be interested in anything but her phone.

Why am I surprised?

Babs tried to look at the scenery, but the windows were dirty, and the pouring rain didn't help. She checked out the stock market on her phone, but that only depressed her.

I should have sold last month.

Instead, she focused her attention on the conductor, a man her age with a well-rounded middle who was waking a shabbily dressed guy, sleeping on the last seat in the car.

"Jake, you have to stop using the train as your home," said the conductor. "There are shelters for you to go to. Show me a ticket or get off."

This Jake must be clever, but he needs to find another train to sleep on.

At the next stop, a young, red-headed, pregnant woman barely maneuvered her three toddlers up the steps to the second-floor seating.

This woman is a candidate for abortion or tying her tubes. Babs! You should be ashamed of yourself. Everyone has a story.

"Mom, do you have any water?"

Babs shifted her attention back to her daughters and dug into her bag. A stocky, bald man seated across from them offered Stacy a bottle of water. Babs quickly handed it back to him. She held up one from her bag and thanked him.

He probably meant no harm, but in today's world, who knows?

They disembarked at Union Station and took the escalator up to Adams Street, right by the Chicago River. Luckily, the rain had stopped, and a sliver of sun peeked through the fluffy white clouds. They walked past the former Sears Tower, now called Willis Tower, where Stacy had been the only one willing to stand out on the sky deck on the 108th floor.

She's always the adventurous one.

The theater on Randolph Street required masks, something they had to get used to again. An architectural gem created in 1926 with a look reminiscent of the Palace of Versailles in France, the Cadillac was one of Chicago's showplaces with decorative mirrors, 2,500 cushy red seats, wood and gold-trimmed walls, and marble stairs. Since being renovated in the 90s, it had been reestablished as one of Chicago's finest landmarks.

The show did not disappoint any of them. They walked out of the theater full of questions, though, as Stacy hummed *Everything's Alright,* and Lori did *Superstar*. Much to their surprise, Aunt Lizzie ran into the middle of the street and waved her arms to hail a cab. The driver stopped just short of running her over and wasn't happy about taking them on such a short ride to the Greek Islands Restaurant. Babs gave him a good tip to make up for the inconvenience. She still couldn't believe that Lizzie had acted so recklessly.

"Why did you do that?"

Aunt Lizzie looked a little shaken up.

"I knew we would never get a cab competing with the show crowd, and truthfully, I thought I was younger than I am. I almost fell in front of that cab."

The restaurant on Halsted Street in Greektown was one of the girls' favorites. Stacy and Lori each had their favorites.

"It's the saganaki," said Lori. "I love that flaming cheese."

"Yeah, me, too," said Stacy, "but I love it even more when the waiters shout 'Opaa' when they bring us the food."

I love the spinach and feta cheese pie. And no one has bread like this place!

The decor reminded them of the Mediterranean, with ocean-painted walls, blue wooden chairs, and white tablecloths.

When they finally slowed down from eating their favorite foods, Lori had questions for her mother.

"Okay, Mom, tell us what we just saw. I loved the music, especially *I Don't Know How to Love Him.*"

How could she? She's 17!

"Lori, the sixties were full of protests, and the seventies meant that people needed to finally accept changes in civil rights and because of the feminism movement. 1973 brought us Roe v. Wade. Plays and movies tried to portray this history. Andre Lloyd Weber and Tim Rice tried to portray Jesus, Judas, and the other characters from the New Testament as human beings in today's world. They show Mary Magdalene as being in love with Jesus, which freaked out the Catholics way more than the Jews. They wanted to make it a contemporary story with the same problems we are dealing with in our own lives. What did you see?"

"Mom, your explanation helps, but I think I need to read the New Testament to understand the whole story. The Jewish Bible doesn't even mention Jesus."

Stacy looked up from her phone long enough to chime in.

"Dummy, this story happened after Moses, which is when our Bible was written."

She grabbed another slice of bread and wasted no time making it disappear. Lizzie looked up from her plate of fish, obviously unhappy.

"I think this play is religious blasphemy that will stir up anti-Semitism. I felt like we were back in the seventies. At least it doesn't have the nudity of that *Hair.*"

Stacy nearly spit up her bread.

"Wait. What? Nudity in a play?"

Babs smiled at Stacy and turned her attention to her cousin.

"Lizzie, you think everything stirs up anti-Semitism. You listen to your mother too much. Tillie told me that the rallies for abortion rights would stir up antisemitism."

Lizzie didn't reply. Stacy and Lori looked surprised. Babs had never spoken to her like that. Babs reached for Lizzie's hand.

"I'm sorry. I get carried away with Shirley and her calls and texts." Lizzie laughed.

"So did your mother. Shirley ran her life after she divorced your father."

Fifty years later, and nothing has changed. Maybe things are worse now. We were a divided nation back then and we still are. Only now, the internet puts it all out in the open.

The waitress boxed their leftovers and added some more crusty rolls. Babs and the girls kissed Aunt Lizzie goodbye and walked to Union Station. Two sleepy girls rested on the ride home while Babs tried to read.

I could write my own family saga.

Chapter Twenty

Babs slept in on Sunday morning until Lassie came crashing through the door, hopped up on her bed, and snuggled on top of her. Stacy and Lori were close behind and plopped down on the other side of the bed. Mark was long gone, getting breakfast ready downstairs. Babs yawned, pushed down her gold-patterned comforter, and sat up.

"What's up?"

"We're wondering what plans we have for the Fourth of July," Stacy said. "After three years of marching with the school band in the Highland Park parade, I'm sick of it. I refused to volunteer again, especially since I'm starting high school. Could we skip it and go somewhere?"

"Truthfully girls, I haven't thought about it. I've been busy with my father's estate. I'm sure you two have something in mind."

Lori and Stacy giggled.

"Joanie's family is going to a resort in Lake Geneva, Wisconsin, called the Grand Geneva," Stacy said. "Could we join them?"

Babs grinned at Lori.

"I bet that's good with you, too. Will someone named Josh also be there? Let's check with Dad. Jill's family will have to do the parade without us this year."

Babs slipped out of bed, peed, did a quick brush and grabbed her blue bathrobe and matching slippers. In record time, she marched downstairs with her girls, ready to feast on Mark's delicious pancakes.

The banging of pots and pans and the aroma of strong coffee greeted Babs and the girls as the three of them bounded into the kitchen and asked him about the Fourth.

"If that's what you want to do, it's fine with me," Mark said. "Sad to miss the parade and the pancake house because you know, they've been a tradition of ours for years."

"Maybe we'll start a new tradition, Dad," said Lori.

Yeah, you mean a new tradition, named Josh?

Mark flipped chocolate chip pancakes off the pan and onto plates. Syrup and freshly squeezed orange juice were already on the table.

"Babs, you better check if we can get last-minute hotel rooms."

Babs nodded. Before they enjoyed their breakfast, she called the hotel while Stacy texted Joannie and Lori texted Josh, assuming their mom would find rooms.

Lassie barked and Babs laughed.

"Thank you, Lassie. You're right. We'll need a good dog sitter if we're going to leave you at home."

"Mom," said Stacy. "Lassie hates firecrackers."

"I know. They make him so jumpy, so we'll find someone who can keep him calm."

Babs motioned for everyone to keep quiet as she spoke to the hotel.

"How do you like that? A family cancelled. Someone got Covid, and they have a suite available with two bedrooms. We're in luck!"

Lori made a show of being disappointed and pointed to her sister.

"You mean I have to share a room with her?"

Stacy held up her fork at Lori.

"I'm just kidding! Let's eat!"

With the Fourth on a Monday, they had a three-day vacation. An hour later, they were packing up the car with multiple bags and cases. Mark only had a small backpack.

"We're only going for three days, and it's just sixty miles from home. If you forget something, we can come back. Why are you taking so much stuff?"

"Dad, we're three females going on vacation. Why are you asking such a silly question?"

Babs threw another suitcase in the back, along with containers of water and snacks.

"We women need several changes of clothes a day. Really, Mark, I can't understand how you can wear the same shirt two days in a row."

Mark shut up, thoroughly outnumbered, as usual.

He could probably wear the same one all week.

The Grand Geneva was once a Playboy Club. Now, it was a family resort situated on 1,300 acres of woods, lakes, and rolling hills in Lake Geneva, Wisconsin. The moment they dropped their luggage in the modern, silver-and-white decorated suite, everyone scattered. Mark hit the golf course, Stacy joined her friends at the water park, and Lori went to Josh's cottage. Joanie's mother took off on a hike, so Babs, in her new black swimsuit, wasted no time securing a blue lounge chair facing the extra-large pool. There was something for everyone. She had a new book called *Women on Fire* and planned to relax and ignore the mess her father had left behind with Jim, and her new brother. She was also determined to forget about the abortion crisis for a few days, as well as Aunt Tillie's party and her insistence that they take a family bus trip to the old building in South Shore.

We will probably all get killed.

By the time Monday the Fourth arrived, everyone was worn out from all the non-stop activities and the abundance of food, but they were tan, a little sunburned, and happy. Stacy had won a few trophies and stuffed animals from the many games she played at the carnival, along with bags of clothes and chokes from her shopping trips. Lori and Josh seemed exhausted from trying to avoid each other's families as much as possible. Apparently, they had done an excellent job because no one hardly saw them all weekend.

Babs became hooked on the spa. It was at least three years since she had enjoyed a real massage and a pedicure. Due to Covid, she had been afraid to go. Joanie's mom encouraged her to pamper herself.

It feels so good, I am coming back as soon as possible. This place is not far from home.

Mark found an interesting museum in town. The girls went along reluctantly at first, only to be the last to leave. Lori pointed out a display about Josh's grandfather, and Joanie's mother was sure that as a young girl she had gone to the dentist who donated to the museum's antique dental office.

Lori was amused.

"Did he treat you with a drill from 1900?"

Stacy thought the corner fudge shop was the best thing in Lake Geneva. She even shared some of the chocolate, chocolate chip fudge.

Oh my God, she's had too much sun. She's sharing!

All through the weekend there was no rain at all, so they enjoyed every bit of the good weather. The night before the Fourth, they watched high-pitched, exploding red, white, and blue fireworks that sprayed across the sky, dazzling the children and adults who crowded together to watch from chairs and blankets on the lush green fields of the golf course.

Early the next morning, they packed up and headed to the restaurant. Babs ordered scrambled eggs from the regular menu while the rest of her family waited in line for the buffet. Stacy loaded her plate with a cheese omelet, chocolate chip pancakes, a bagel and lox, and an assortment of pastries.

"You'll never eat all of that," Lori said. "You're just wasting food."

Lori's right, but what a great feeling it must be to eat anything you want and as much as you want and not gain an ounce.

Josh joined them. His plate was fuller than Stacy's, but he finished every bite.

"I know you plan to leave soon," he said, "but would it be okay if Lori came home with my family this evening?"

Babs shrugged.

"Maybe. Let's enjoy breakfast first and then we'll see."

Chapter Twenty-One

For some reason she couldn't explain, Babs wanted to go home together as a family. She had expected to meet Josh's parents during the weekend, but it never happened. Mark knew his father from growing up in Lake Forest, but Babs ran in different groups than Josh's mother.

Outside the restaurant, a gigantic television played in the lobby. As Babs and her family got up to leave, they noticed people racing toward the screen. As they moved in that direction, they wondered what could be causing such a commotion. When they got close enough to see the TV, they heard voices shaking and wailing.

"I don't believe it, not in Highland Park!"

"It's a shooting!"

"Oh, my God, Not another one!"

"A mass murderer? There must be a mistake."

Everyone was horrified by what they were seeing. Most people looked shocked, and some were already in tears. The biggest emotion, palpable to anyone in the lobby, was fear.

Babs twisted her hair in her fingers and held on tight to Stacy.

"Mom, those kids running with their musical instruments would have been in my band."

"Oh my God, are you kidding?"

"No, not at all. Look! That's our mixed Highland Park/Lake Forest band. Are they really being shot at? I'm sure I know some of them. I mean, I know I do! Mom, what is happening in Highland Park? I don't understand!"

Babs and her family stood in shock like everyone else while the story unfolded. According to the news report, a rooftop sniper was firing dozens of shots as the parade unfolded in Highland Park.

This is way too close to home.

The cameras showed people dazed everywhere, wandering around as if they couldn't tell if they were hearing firecrackers or gunshots. Many of them seemed to be running around haphazardly, not knowing where it was safe to hide.

My neighboring town is turning into a war zone.

The hotel guests and restaurant patrons were frozen in front of the television. They watched in horror as the live footage showed people running past stores and restaurants, all familiar to Babs and her family. The camera showed deserted chairs and backpacks, as people ran for cover, wherever and however, they could. Some were hiding behind cars while others sped off on their bicycles. A news anchor could be heard, narrating what they could, but no one seemed to be sure of what was going on.

The camera soon focused on blood-covered bodies lying on the streets and sidewalks they knew so well. They heard screams of "Oh God" and prayers in English and Spanish.

Babs stared at a bloody body in front of her favorite meeting place, Walker's Pancake House. People rushed from one end of the street to the next, screaming, with blood pouring from wounds. Women grabbed their children and ran. Pedestrians watched stupefied as blood spattered windows and storefronts.

The next few hours were a blur. As Babs and the family remained glued to the television, they were on the phone, calling and texting everyone they knew to make sure they were safe and sound. Friends and family reached out to them, not knowing they were out of town. When it was hard to locate certain people, they panicked. Mark's sister called from Italy, shocked and worried about Stacy.

"I was afraid she was in the marching band."

They assured her that she was not there and safe with her family.

Thank God.

It was too early to tell if they knew any of the victims. So far, they hadn't heard of anyone familiar being shot, but a few friends had fled and hidden in one of the stores on Central Street. Most of them were closed for the holiday, but the few that were open were filled with people, petrified to go outside.

A tiny blonde woman standing next to Babs looked familiar. She had been sitting near them in the restaurant and was watching things unfold on the television when she suddenly rushed out of the resort. Babs wondered if she had seen someone she knew on TV and sped off to Highland Park hospital to find out if they were there.

We could get a phone call any minute about someone we know.

American families had been dealing with mass shootings for many years and some had protested and signed petitions for new gun laws, with little success to show for their efforts. But until tragedy hit close to home, it seems abstract.

Now, it was an entirely new paradigm for Babs and her family. Highland Park was literally close to home, just a small suburb away. It was the North Shore hub of Jewish activities, full of temples, kosher butchers, and the last of a dying breed of kosher-style delis. One store still made its own bagels, and you could get a corned beef or pastrami sandwich on rye with a piece of kishka right next door.

Babs twisted her hair in her fingers. She knew every street and store the journalists were talking about. She was in shock.

"Mark, let's go home."

She had gathered her girls and wouldn't let them out of her sight. She took out a tissue to wipe her watery eyes. At first, she was angry, then afraid and now she felt overwhelmed.

"Mark, please."

"Honey, it's a mess. The roads will be blocked. Let's wait a while and hope they capture the gunman soon."

They managed to get back into their suite and immediately turned on the television. Once Stacy felt sure that none of her friends had been hurt or killed, her old instincts returned.

"Can we order room service?"

"No. I don't want anyone coming in here," Babs said.

Mark tossed a menu to his girls and plopped on the bed.

"Come on. Calm down, Babs. We're sixty miles away, and the authorities are sure it was a lone gunman."

Tears ran down her face.

"I can't lose anyone else. My mother is gone, and now my father, too."

"It's going to be okay."

Babs leaned into her husband.

"Girls, figure out what you want to order."

"Babs, come on. Let's just be grateful that we are here instead of in Highland Park, thanks to Stacy. We'll go home soon and help our neighbors and friends."

The girls watched their mother get up and head to the bathroom. She stopped and smiled. "Order me a hamburger, please."

I can't believe I'm hungry. I guess we eat when we're upset.

Babs washed her face and put on a little makeup. When her mother died, Aunt Tillie had quickly made her get out of bed.

"When your family needs you, Babs, you become a good actress."

Time to win an Oscar.

Mark assured Babs that it was safe to go home. The police had reported that the lone sniper, a 21-year-old, male, Highland Park resident, had killed seven people and injured more than 40 others. The suspect was now in jail, and the news confirmed the police announcement that no one else was involved.

The old neighborhood in South Shore isn't our only danger zone.

Chapter Twenty-Two

As the horror of the shooting in Highland Park lingered, Babs, Lori, and Stacy brought food to victims' families and attended more funerals than they ever imagined possible in such a short time. The suburbs on the North Shore of Chicago were small enough that even if you didn't know any of the victims, you probably knew someone who did.

Stacy was particularly shaken up because she knew two band participants. She and Joanie brought them homemade chocolate chip cookies and listened to them talk about the shooting. When Babs picked up the girls, she brought them into her kitchen and asked Joanie about Stacy.

"Was she a good listener, instead of all talk?"

"Mom!"

Stacy started to sulk, and Joanie smiled.

"She tried."

"How are your friends doing?" Babs said. "It must have been very scary being shot at."

"Harry was upset that he lost his clarinet and one of his shoes, but his sister, who was in the crowd, wouldn't join us," Joanie said. "They weren't hurt, but they were scared. At first, everyone thought it was firecrackers, because it was the Fourth of July. When they realized it was gunshots, they ran into the clothing store."

"I don't blame them," Babs said. "We were scared just watching it on television."

They heard a horn beep. Joanie stood up and looked out the window.

"My mom's here. Bye."

As she left, Babs turned to Stacy.

"Honey, you aren't talking. That isn't like you. How are you doing?"

"I'm good, Mom. It's just that I won't have anything to do with bands, parades, or rallies anymore. No way."

She took two cookies and left the room. Babs looked up the scheduled meetings with the school social workers and wondered if Stacy would even go to them.

She isn't herself, but she probably won't go. Mark will say give her time. Stop worrying.

Babs looked under the table at Stacy's new shoes and perked up when she heard the television go on in the family room with Stacy's favorite show, *Shark Tank*.

Jill called.

"We're trying to get signatures on a petition for gun control. Will you join us?"

"Where?"

Please don't say it will be at our usual place, The Pancake House.

That was the last place Babs wanted to go, close to the site of the shooting. Fortunately, they met at the Cubby Hole near Deerfield and spent four hours gathering signatures on the petition to be sent to the Illinois General Assembly.

I'm spending more hours now on gun control than abortion.

She and Lori had been at a rally for gun control a few days earlier. Between Texas, Highland Park, and the relentless crime in Chicago, people were fed up. On her way home, she stopped in Highland Park. Without saying a word to each other, they stood with several others and stared at the stuffed animals, poems, flowers, and prayer books that had been placed near the makeshift memorial.

Babs came back the next day to persuade more people to sign the petition.

Charlene Wexler

Yes, people kill people, but people with machine guns can kill more people much faster.

Chapter Twenty-Three

A summer downpour wasn't unusual on a sunny Chicago day. Babs ran from her car with a piece of newspaper over her newly done hairdo.

I should keep an umbrella in the car like Mom always did.

She hated traveling downtown, but Larry said he needed a personal conference. She ran into his law office before the secretary had a chance to direct her. She had become a regular and was no longer afraid of how Larry seemed to try to intimidate her.

Babs removed her coat and shook off the rain like Lassie. She sat down and pushed her chair closer to Larry.

"He wants to sue us, Babs. If he does that, it could take years before the estate is settled."

"Who?"

"Byron, your new brother."

"Larry, is his mother still alive?"

"No, but he has a notarized letter from her saying Ronnie is his father, plus a more recent DNA test."

"I remember her. Dad took us to London several times, and she took care of us. Byron was never there. I would love to see a picture of his mother. My aunt thinks someone by that name once lived in Chicago near the family building."

Larry shook his head.

"She would be too old to be Byron's mother. I can't believe Ronnie didn't tell me about Byron."

He opened a cupboard and poured some brandy into a crystal glass.

"Babs, do you want a drink? What you are saying will only help him. Remind me not to put you on the stand if this ends up in court. I think he said his grandmother lived in Chicago. How would your aunt know?"

"My great aunt, Tillie Paul, knows everyone Jewish from Chicago, dead or alive."

"Your aunt is *the* Tillie Paul! Are you kidding? She's still alive?"

Babs looked puzzled and smiled.

"At one time, she ran the West Side. Did you know that? She and the judge. Ask her about it, Babs. I'm serious."

He shook his head and asked her again if she wanted a drink.

"No alcohol, thanks, but I could use a coffee."

Larry pressed a button and a coffee arrived in record time—black, as she liked it.

"I'm not sure what you mean about Aunt Tillie. She is going to be a hundred next month. Did you know that?"

Larry gulped down the whiskey like it was water.

"I can't believe Ronnie never told me Byron was his son. When I visited London, only Sophia was there. I always thought we were honest with each other. We go back over fifty years. Last month, when I went to see Ron, he couldn't recognize me. That hurt the most."

"Larry, I don't want to go to court with Byron. I know my father, and I accept that Byron is my half-brother. It is what it is. I'm just happy that ten other half-brothers or half-sisters haven't shown up."

Larry laughed. He continued pacing back and forth while Babs drank her coffee. Then, he sat down and leaned in toward her.

"Jim must agree with you. Can you get him to see me? Also, my job is to sell all of Ronnie's properties. That includes the house in Glencoe and the townhouse in London. Everything in the Glencoe house belongs to the two of you, but the townhouse belongs to the estate. Clean it out with your brother, so we can stop paying the enormous bills to keep it going. Ron left money to Charles and Dorothy, so don't feel sorry for them. Babs, we would rather not sell stocks in today's down market. The housing market is still moving, though the timeshare in Aspen wasn't a good investment. We will lose money there."

"My mother hated Aspen. She said that was where Dad took all his girlfriends."

Larry nodded.

"Yes, he did. She was right."

Before leaving the office, Babs glanced up at the picture on his desk of a young, tall, thin Larry with a full head of black hair, and a young, black-haired, dimpled Ronnie. They had been fraternity brothers at The University of Illinois and then law school classmates at Harvard. That was the only picture on Larry's desk. He had been married and divorced with no kids. He was always there for Babs's father, balling him out of many dubious and potentially embarrassing situations.

Hard to believe Larry didn't know about Byron!

Babs stopped halfway out the door and turned back to look at Larry.

"Did you like Dad?"

Larry looked up from his desk and hesitated.

"Babs, I loved Ronnie from the first day I met him, even though he made me crazy."

She twisted her hair in her fingers and left.

I don't know how to take his answer.

Babs knew she had to deal with her brother.

At least he's done with anger management.

That 30-day seminar was his punishment for hitting Byron. She decided to call Trish. Maybe with the money from her father, she and Jim would get back together. He needed help, and so far, he hadn't allowed Babs to provide any support.

One of us must get through to him.

She pulled into the garage, slid out of the car, and headed to the backyard, where she could hear Lassie barking. Mark was on a ladder, picking apples off the tree he had planted several years ago and throwing them to a giggling Stacy.

The apples that fall on the ground are getting bruised.

Babs didn't say a word because she could see that they were having so much fun. She waved and backed up into the kitchen.

She was chopping vegetables when they came in later, carrying a large, wicker basket full of apples. Mark was beaming.

"After dinner, Stacy and I will make some apple pie. Right, Stacy?"

"Yes, Dad."

Stacy started to set the table for dinner while she texted her friends.

I still can't believe how she can multi-task. If I tried that, I would probably drop the plates and text the wrong person.

Mark watched her, too, and laughed. He stepped back into the kitchen to tease Babs.

"So, How was the meeting? Are we filthy rich yet?"

As Babs told Mark about the meeting, her voice grew louder and full of agitation.

"Dad left me so much mishigas to deal with, particularly cleaning out the house."

"Babs, we will help you. How about the whole family goes to the house on Sunday? Leave your brother a message, let him decide what he wants to do, and then forget him. You can't take care of everyone. Hello?"

Babs shrugged. Mark smiled and turned to leave.

"I'm putting the salmon on the grill."

Babs stared at her husband. He had a way of uncomplicating things that she found difficult. Maybe it came from living in a family of three brothers and two sisters.

Like my aunts and uncles and cousins experienced in the famous family building.

"Where is Lori?" Babs said.

"Upstairs with a bad stomach," said Mark.

Babs went up to check on her daughter, who just wanted to be left alone.

Probably time for her period.

Babs came back into the kitchen and watched Mark and Stacy peel apples and prepare their store-bought pie shells.

"Don't let Aunt Tillie know you aren't making the pies from scratch."

"I liked rolling dough with her, Mom, but Dad says it takes too long."

"Stacy, do you know what is wrong with Lori? She missed school Friday, and she's sick again today, and she wouldn't talk to me."

Stacy shrugged and popped a cinnamon-sugared apple slice into her mouth.

Chapter Twenty-Four

Babs let Larry know that they were going to the house on Sunday. He sent her an appraisal of most of the important things there. She was disappointed to find out the car, plus the Picasso and the Chagall, were on loan from the law firm, and even though the furniture was in excellent shape, it was old and not worth much.

Larry told her the money from selling the house would go into the estate and eventually to her and Jim, while the London townhouse would go to Byron. The Glencoe house would bring in more money, especially if they found the right buyer.

Babs texted Trish, and without telling anyone, she texted Byron.

"I hope you are healed. I'd like to get to know you, as we have genes in common."

He texted back.

"Thanks. I have no physical scars. We should get to know each other."

It's a start.

She would wait a while before she tried again.

Trish texted back.

"Jim wants nothing from his father. Let us know when the house is going on the market. Maybe I will get him there beforehand. I could use a good vacuum and some kitchen pots."

Mark, Babs, Lori, and Stacy drove to the house in Mark's ancient but reliable blue Chevy van. As they drove down the fancy Sheridan Road, Mark began to sing.

"Here comes the Beverly Hillbillies!"

He was in a fun mood until they got there. Then he sat down on a bench overlooking the lake, uninterested in going inside.

"Babs, you and the girls decide what you want. Okay? These furnishings are too uppity for me. How much are they selling the house for?"

"I think they are asking two and a half million. Do you want to buy it?"

She rolled her eyes.

"I couldn't live here again. I can't even believe I once did. We won't have Dad's money for a year or more, and we have no guarantee of how much we'll end up getting."

Babs stood in her father's gigantic, organized closet with what looked like at least 500 expensive suits.

Even if Mark were the same size, he would never have a place to wear them.

She offered them to Charles, who thanked her and declined. She wanted to find someone who could use the suits and thought it would be a shame if they went to Goodwill.

Lori was in heaven, looking through her grandfather's library.

"Mom, how many books can I take? I wish we could take home all these shelves."

"They're built in, Honey. You can take as many books as you want, but where will you store them?"

Babs looked around for something to put the books in. She walked over to her father's closet, pulled out a suitcase and gave it to Lori.

"You can come back with boxes and take more."

Lori turned toward her mother with hands on her hips.

"Mom, these books should go to a library or some schools. They're in perfect shape, and there must be two or three hundred. Please don't just sell them or give them away."

"I'll talk to Larry, and you can find some good places where we can donate them."

Babs turned to her younger daughter.

"Stacy, Why are you sitting here with Dad?"

"Nothing for me unless you can move the pool to our house."

Babs glanced out at the pool, which had only been built about ten years ago.

I can't remember a time when it ever had water.

Surrounding the pool were 20 perfectly shaped evergreens. Babs pictured her father in his heyday, walking with the gardener to make sure the trees were uniform.

He was such a perfectionist.

The tree she loved most was a big old elm on the path down to the beach. Its girth was massive, and the branches reached out close to the water. She liked to hide by it with a book.

God, when I was young, I liked anyplace where I could hide.

Babs understood how Mark and Stacy felt. Removing things from the house seemed like stealing from a hotel, not a house with memories, like when her mother died. Everything she kept then had a history—things she lived with, aromas she used to inhale, plates they ate on, books her mom loved, antiques from the family building, jewelry, picture albums, cologne, clothes mom wore, and the Gucci briefcase her father had given her mother when she graduated law school—all good memories.

In her father's place, this rich man's sterile mansion, there was none of that. Babs packed pots and pans and the robot vacuum for Trish, the Lalique crystal pieces for herself, and boxes of papers from her father's office. She offered his clothes and some of his personal things to Charles and leftover kitchen items to Dorothy. To Mark's disappointment, there were no tools or gardening equipment. Those jobs had all been done by outside help.

Babs planned to ask Larry about the car, even though Mark thought it was too old and would cost a fortune when they needed parts. They took the swing from the patio and two of the expensive, padded blue lounge chairs. She would come back alone or with Trish for a once-over before the house went on the market.

Larry has all of Dad's business and law papers.

As a lawyer, Babs might want to see or save some of them. She and Jim needed to meet Larry at the bank downtown to empty Dad's safe deposit box.

She wanted her father's oak antique roll-top desk with its cubby holes and shiny brass knobs. It was always locked in her youth. She imagined it still filled with the treasures he brought back from those business trips, such as Russian dolls or fudge from Mackinac Island.

Babs found the key in his top dresser drawer. She was tempted to open it, but she decided to wait. One time, he had hidden a diamond bracelet in it. Her mother found it and thanked him, although it was most likely meant for a girlfriend.

Mark and Charles loaded the desk into the van. They were ready to go, so Babs approached Charles.

"Please tell Dorothy we are leaving. We will keep you both informed."

Charles hesitated.

"You can't leave, Babs. Not yet. Dorothy has been busy preparing a bistro lunch, just like she did when Mr. Greenspan was in good health. Please come to the back patio. She will be so disappointed if you leave."

Mark and Stacy gave Babs a "help" look, but she ignored them.

"Of course, we'll stay."

She shrugged and waved them on. They walked around to the back of the house and sat down on blue wooden plank chairs next to a table set for four. Delicate rose-flowered cups and matching plates sat on a lace, white-linen tablecloth. Their napkins were wrapped inside China rings next to sterling silver forks, knives, spoons, and water in crystal goblets. A single rose in a white porcelain vase topped off the lovely setting.

Babs appreciated the effort Dorothy had made and let her know it. The table on the patio overlooking the lake couldn't have been more perfect. As they watched the water on the sandy beach, Stacy pointed to a seagull who dived in, looking for his lunch.

Dorothy served them a mixed green salad with tomato and goat cheese with a mushroom quiche and fruit, along with homemade muffins. Charles poured white wine and reminded them that there was a wine closet in the basement.

Babs watched Stacy sip the wine.

"It's good. But I like Passover wine better."

Babs smiled at Dorothy.

"You've outdone yourself, Dorothy. I feel like I'm in a French bistro."

Dorothy's face lit up.

"Thank you, Babs. My pleasure. I packed the dishes, silverware, and crystal. I will add this service when you are done. You should have these fine things in your home. There are two other China sets, you know. Perhaps your brother will want one."

Babs rose from her chair and hugged Dorothy.

"You should take one of them, and I'll take the other one for Jim. What will you and Charles do when the house is sold?"

"We've been waiting a long time to retire in Green Bay, where our grandchildren live."

Mark laughed.

"So, all these years you've been secret Packer fans!"

Charles laughed and nodded.

"Yes. Big fan. Dorothy never bothered with sports."

After lunch, Stacy and Lori ran down to the beach. They took their shoes off and trudged along, picking up feathers, pebbles, a water bottle, and a children's whistle. Stacy danced around in the moving water. Lori put a foot in and out, as she declared it too cold.

"I wish the pool were full and working."

As Mark and Babs sat at the lunch table, watching their girls, he turned to Babs.

"Why did you hate this place so much? It's like heaven."

Babs twirled her hair in her fingers.

"I told you how strict and abusive my father used to be. We were out of place here. I had no friends. Most families were from old Christian money, and we weren't accepted. I was ignored at school, and the other kids always whispered about me. For Dad's sake, Mom tried to be a society lady, but it didn't work for her. I loved living in Northbrook later. Aunt Tillie used to say, 'Birds of a feather need to stay together.' "

"We come from different feathers," Mark said.

He looked at Babs with a smirk. She gripped his hand and squeezed it tight.

"I'd say our feathers work well together."

Chapter Twenty-Five

Three days later, Babs received a text from Byron.

"I never understood Dad. Sometimes, he was nice to us, and other times as mean as possible. I thought he was like that because I was the bastard son while his real children lived across the ocean."

Babs was delighted that they were making a connection, and she felt for Byron. She texted him right back to let him know that this was the personality of their shared father.

"Besides being a Type A personality, our father was probably bipolar and should have been put on medication."

Byron texted back a week later and asked if they were keeping the house. Babs was about to call Larry to discuss the matter when he reached out to her with welcome news. Byron had dropped the lawsuit, and Larry could now try to get things moving. Babs was relieved. She had initially texted Byron, hoping he would back off, but now, that barrier to a possible relationship had disappeared. She could text Byron because she genuinely wanted to get to know him.

No matter what, he's family.

He began by answering her basic questions about him and his family.

"I am a gay designer. I have a partner, no children, but I do have a large extended family on my mother's side."

"Did Dad know?"

"Know what?"

"That you were, you know, gay."

"What a question."

"I know. Sorry. It's a sensitive topic."

"No need to apologize. I'm a big boy."

"I didn't mean it like that."

"It's okay, Babs."

"You know, my mother's first cousin was a gay designer. Dad reluctantly allowed him to come to my parents' wedding, but he wouldn't let his lover to join him."

"Ouch."

"Yeah. Later, in the eighties, my cousin died of AIDS."

"Sorry, Babs. We all lost so many during that time."

"Yes, we did."

"But to answer your question. No, our father did not know I was gay."

Babs loved their easy back-and-forth. Their father was an extremely straight conservative who believed that girlfriends were a man's right, but that being gay went against nature. She was relieved that they shared this common understanding of their father.

"Babs, you need to come to London. I can show you where we live, not just the tourist attractions. My mom lived on a farm outside of London. Her family would love to meet you."

"Maybe this fall when the girls are back in school."

"Please bring the girls. I would love to show them London."

As Babs went into the kitchen to figure out what to make for dinner, her phone rang. After taking the call, she turned to Lori, who was busy reading.

"Want to join me at an abortion rally in Wisconsin? They have strict rules there against it, you know. Jill is picking me up tomorrow morning."

"Mom, I'm done with abortion rallies."

Lori slammed her book down and ran upstairs. Babs looked at Stacy, who shrugged. Babs went upstairs to talk with her daughter.

"Lori, I can tell that something isn't right. Do you need a doctor?"

"Mom, please leave me alone. I need to work some things out on my own."

Early the next day, just as the sun was rising, there was a knock at the door. Babs looked out the window and ran downstairs. She was still in her pink Chanel bathrobe and matching slippers as she answered the door.

"Josh, you're here early! It's only 6:30. Does Lori know you're coming now?"

"She should. We planned to drive to Lake Geneva early and go boating on the lake. It's only a day trip, and I have to do some fundraising with my parents tomorrow."

Josh stood on the front porch in his high school shirt, blue jeans, and a baseball cap.

"Come inside. I'll get Lori. Congratulations to your dad. I hear he's running for State Representative."

Babs went upstairs.

Something is amiss. Lori wouldn't forget a day trip with Josh.

Babs hugged Lori as she came out of the bathroom in her two-piece shorty pajamas. She looked pale.

"You don't look so good, my dear. What's wrong? Josh is waiting downstairs, you know. You guys are supposed to be going to Lake Geneva, but maybe you should stay home."

"No, I'll be all right, Mom. I have to go today."

Lori picked up speed as she went into her closet to grab some clothes.

Babs heard Mark and Josh laughing and talking about sports, so she went back into her master bath and showered.

Something isn't right with my Lori. She's been acting weird, sleeping a lot, having stomach trouble, and not talking to me. After this weekend, I'm taking her to Dr. Shapiro.

By the time Babs was done in the bathroom, Lori and Josh were on their way. It was the fourth time they'd gone to Lake Geneva over the summer. Lori was usually enthusiastic about going, especially now that she was taking care of seven-year-olds all day, which could be taxing.

Babs fixed herself a cup of coffee.

Hopefully, Lori is okay, and it's just something about her job that's bothering her.

Babs had to stop speculating and get ready for the rally in Wisconsin. Jill was picking her up in 40 minutes. She pulled out her phone and checked the weather. Blue jeans and light jacket. They would be outside of the Madison capitol, which was a beautiful state house in a college town. She hoped she would have time to buy some of Wisconsin's homemade cheeses. They were so much better than what the grocery stores sold.

The Supreme Court now gave states the right to determine whether abortion would be legal inside their borders. Wisconsin was going back to an 1849 law that banned *all* abortions. As a result, Babs and her friends could be busier than her mother and Shirley were back in 1973, especially if they had to rally separately in each state and take on each state legislature.

In Illinois, where abortion was legal, the number of out-of-state patients was soaring. Her group's next rally would be in Springfield, the state capital. They would call for additional funding for clinics and Planned Parenthood organizations.

I need to get the girls involved. This fight is for them!

They had grown up in a world untouched by reproductive issues and problems of women's equality, at least in their suburban bubble. Elections were only a few months away. All the rights that had been won years ago could be taken away in a hurry.

Charlene Wexler

I hope they're smart enough, and lucky enough, to never need an abortion.

Chapter Twenty-Six

There was a chill in the early morning air and Josh had the top down on his beloved convertible.

After sliding into the passenger seat, Lori pulled a sweater out of her bag and pulled it over her sleeveless, pale blue shirt.

She hardly talked. Her mind kept going over the conversation she knew she had to have with him. Her heart raced. The hour-and-a-half drive went slowly. Music blasted from the radio as they turned off route 12 and rolled into downtown Lake Geneva.

"Lori, do you want to stop for breakfast?"

"No, I'm not feeling very good."

"You've been sick a lot lately. We missed Roger's pool party last weekend."

"I told you to go by yourself."

Josh tapped the steering wheel in time with the music, while Lori stared out the window. What was supposed to be a romantic getaway was turning into something else entirely. As they pulled up to the cottage, Lori felt her body tense up. She didn't want to go inside. In her mind, what she used to consider their romantic love nest had not turned into a rundown place of evil, the same place that had ruined her life.

She barely made it to the downstairs bathroom before she vomited all over the floor. Josh looked in, turned white, and backed away quickly.

"Shit, Lori. I hope you don't have Covid. My dad will kill me if I miss his campaign event next weekend."

She moved away from the toilet, grabbed a towel, and washed her face. She could barely look at Josh.

"I'd rather have Covid than be pregnant."

Josh looked terrified as he turned to face her.

"Oh, fuck! Fuck! Pregnant!?! You're kidding, aren't you? Aren't you? Tell me this is a sick joke."

Lori stared at him and shook her head.

"Did you get tested? Maybe you're wrong. You gotta be wrong."

"I've tested, Josh. I'm not stupid. I've missed three periods, and this throwing up is morning sickness."

Tears flowed down her face.

He paced back and forth, seeming to grow more frustrated with each step.

"How could you do this to us? Why weren't you on the pill? "

"How could *I* do this?"

"Yeah, you. This is on you."

"Josh, you told me you had condoms. You told me you loved me. You sure aren't acting like it now."

Lori wanted Josh to hold her, but he looked at her like she was the devil. He talked to himself like she wasn't even there.

"I'm confused right now and frustrated. Shit! Having a baby will ruin my college career, and having an abortion will ruin my father's political chances. He's running a pro-life campaign, you know. I'm only seventeen. I'm too young to have a baby. My dad won't support us. You can be sure of that. I'll have to stay home and work at a meaningless job. My life will be ruined."

Lori stared at Josh and felt her heart sink. Her eyes opened wide.

"You, you, you. What about me? It's *my* body, Josh, and it will be my decision."

"God, Lori, you sound like a stupid commercial for abortion."

"Are you kidding me?"

"You could go away, have the baby, and put it up for adoption."

Josh looked at Lori, hoping she would instantly agree.

"You would only miss a half year of school."

She couldn't believe the way he was talking and acting. It was all about him. She had spent two years thinking she was in love with this selfish person. She went into the bedroom and fell on the bed and let the tears flow. Josh sat down next to her, but he didn't touch her.

"We'll figure it out. Fuck. Stop crying. That won't help."

He got up and paced back and forth with his hands stuck in his pockets.

"I want to go home, Josh."

"Could you clean up the bathroom first?"

Lori was too worn out to be angry at her supposed boyfriend, She took some paper towels and a spray bottle of cleanser from the shelf under the sink. As she scrubbed the floor, more tears ran down her cheeks. Finally, when she felt the bathroom was clean, she found Josh outside, smoking a joint.

"Please take me home."

They drove back in complete silence. Josh kept the top up, as if he were doing Lori a big favor. Her whole body ached, from her head to her toes. Her mother was at a rally for women's rights to abortion. How would she feel when she finds out her 17-year-old unmarried daughter was pregnant?

Josh opened the car door for Lori when they arrived in front of her house. He stood there like a cat, ready to bolt. He didn't offer a touch or a kiss.

"We'll figure something out."

To Lori, his abrupt and callous words sounded like "goodbye and good luck."

Josh's face was expressionless, as if this whole thing was a business problem he had to figure out. To make matters worse, he acted like it was all Lori's fault. In truth, he was the one who had forgotten to use a condom after promising that he would. Babs had suggested using birth control pills, but Lori had refused. She thought that she and Josh could continue playing around caressing each other without going all the way.

When Lori turned to go in, Josh jumped into his car, slammed the door shut, gunned the motor, and raced away. She ran up the driveway, into the house, and up the stairs. No one was home except Lassie, who followed her into her bedroom.

She was scared and feeling desperate. She hoped the test was wrong. But as she reached for a glimmer of hope. Lori knew the result was right. After all, her breasts were fuller, and throwing up in the morning was a pretty sure sign of being pregnant.

No way did she want to talk to her family that night. She put her pajamas on, turned out the light, pulled her down comforter over her head, and pretended to be asleep when her mom poked her head in the door.

Chapter Twenty-Seven

Lori stayed up most of the night, sitting by her bedroom window. The sun was a ball of fire as it crested on the horizon. It was a new day, but the same problem loomed in Lori's mind, and she felt it lurking in her body. Although no one was there to hear her, she spoke out loud, as if she were praying.

"What can I do? I can't feel anything. I feel frozen inside. I should be thinking about my graduation and the prom."

She opened the window. The air was crisp and clean.

"Maybe I should jump out the window. It's only two stories high, though, so it would probably only leave me maimed for life. No baby, but who wants to be paralyzed?"

After Josh dropped her off, he had not called or texted.

"He kept saying we'll work something out. Where is he now? Has he disappeared? How could he, after two years together? After telling me he loved me. He was probably strung out on pot. He's an athlete, about to get a full-ride scholarship, and he smokes so much weed. I wonder what the university would say if they knew."

Lori had tried marijuana once and didn't like the feeling it gave her. She liked the way it smelled, sweet and earthy, but it gave her a headache.

As she thought about Josh and his drug use, Lori felt more tears running down her cheeks. She was surprised she still had any left after crying so much through the night. She blew her nose and wiped her eyes. Her head hurt, and her stomach felt tight.

It was a Sunday morning, and Babs was tired, so she stayed in bed a little longer with Lassie. Mark was already gone, golfing with some friends. Stacy was at a sleepover, and figured that Lori was still at the lake with Josh.

She finally got out of bed to pee and decided to start her day.

Too much to do and never enough time!

She ignored the dishes in the sink and walked out onto the patio, still in her fluffy pink robe, and curled up on a lounge chair with a book and a tall glass of iced tea. Lassie followed and laid down at her side. The rallies had taken a toll on her physically *and* emotionally.

I would love a massage right now.

The temptation was real, but with Covid still around and something new, called monkeypox, Babs was afraid of risking so much close contact. She closed her eyes and fell asleep until she felt someone sitting next to her.

When Babs looked at her daughter's red eyes and poker face, she immediately knew something was wrong. She sat up straight and peered into Lori's eyes, looking for a clue.

"Did you and Josh fight?"

"Oh, Mom, how I wish that was it."

"What's wrong, Sweetheart?"

Lori looked out at the lake.

"I didn't want to tell you, but I have some news. Some bad news."

Babs felt a knot in her stomach. She twisted her hair around in her fingers.

"What have you done, Lori? Are you sick? Are you in trouble? Talk to me."

Babs got up and shook her daughter. She didn't want to hear Lori say the words, but she knew they were coming.

Lori looked away.

"Mom."

"Say it!"

"I'm pregnant, and Josh wants nothing to do with it."

Lassie, sensing something wrong, licked Lori's face. Babs remained still, trying to absorb what Lori had just told her. She knew it was coming, but she was not prepared to hear it out loud.

Not in our family. Please, no. All the rallies, all the petitions, all the talks with politicians. Those were for other families, low-income and not Jewish.

Lori's face was red from crying; her hair was twisted, and her pajama top was all twisted. She needed her mother in such a moment, and Babs felt the same way.

What would Mom do right now?

She twirled her hair against her head, pulled Lori in close to her and held her tight.

How could Lori have been so careless? With all this Roe v. Wade stuff going on, all we've been talking about is birth control and abortion. Why was I so stupid? All the signs were there—lousy stomach, too sick to join the family, not seeing her boy or girlfriends. Now that I'm paying attention, I can see that her breasts are fuller, too.

"Oh, my God, Lori."

"Mom, I'm scared. I told Josh last night, and he acted like I was ruining his life on purpose, like he had nothing to do with it."

Babs took a deep breath.

"Did you take a test, and how far gone are you?"

"How far gone? Mom!"

"Along. How far along are you?"

"I tested positive. I think ten weeks."

Lori looked down at her bare feet.

"What does Josh want you to do?"

Lori sank into her lounge chair.

"Mom, I thought we were in love. Both of us. Both ways. You know, mutual."

Babs nodded, hoping her daughter was right.

"Mom, Josh could only think about himself and his conservative father who is running for office and is totally against abortion. He told me to go away, have the baby, and put it up for adoption, and that he would pay. As if he can just make it all disappear."

"No way, Lori."

"Really, Mom. He never thought of me. Not at all."

Babs was angry, but she tried to be gentle.

"What do you want to do?"

Lori shook her head and shrugged.

"Mom, I don't know. I'm scared!"

"Of course, you are. That's okay."

She squeezed Lori's hand.

"First, I want you to know I love you very much. You made a mistake, Lori, however it happened, but that doesn't matter right now. The most important thing is, you have a loving family here to help you. We've gone to rallies and signed petitions to ensure that girls, I mean young women, in your position can make their own choices. In Illinois, until further notice, you have a choice."

Babs hugged Lori and held her breath to keep from crying out.

I need help.

She knew that if it were up to Mark, she would end up raising their daughter's child.

He needs to know.

Babs thought of Aunt Tillie, who would pray and moan and groan.

"Oh vey!"

Then, they would eat before she offered more of her opinion.

"Jewish girls do not have children out of wedlock."

Babs knew she had to go with Lori to see Shirley.
She'll know what to do.

"Lori, we'll deal with Josh together. I don't know how, not yet, but we will. How dare he abandon you when you need him? He's a kid, like you, but that's just not right."

Lori nodded. Babs twirled her hair in her fingers.

Remember, they are only 17 years old.

Trying to stay calm, Babs took a drink of her iced tea.

"Lori, let me try to get a hold of Shirley. Go take your shower and get dressed. I'll make us some breakfast, and then we'll go visit Shirley in Chicago. She's been dealing with women's issues for the last fifty years. She'll know what to do."

Lori pulled away from her mother.

"Please, Mom, don't tell anyone now. And I can't eat anything."

"Honey, you have some decisions to make, and soon, too, although you're too late for the new abortion pill. But in Illinois, you can get an abortion until week twenty-four."

Lori gulped and nodded.

"I know you want to keep this quiet now, and we will, but Shirley is the best one to talk to and the sooner you figure this out, the better."

Lori shrugged.

"You need to eat something, too. I'll make us something. Go get dressed."

Babs stood at the stove, beating the hell out of three poor eggs.

I need to tell Mark. If we tell Stacy, can she keep quiet?

Chapter Twenty-Eight

Lori and Babs left the house before Mark and Stacy came home. Babs talked all the way downtown while Lori looked out the window. When they arrived at Shirley's condo, she met them at the door. Babs looked around for Rachel.

"Where is Rachel?"

Shirley picked up a newspaper from her kitchen counter and turned to the obituaries. She pointed to one of the columns.

"Rachel's cousin, Lori, just died. You may remember her. They lived in Northbrook when you did. Back in the eighties, her daughter died of leukemia."

Babs turned to Lori.

"You told me nothing could be worse than your pregnancy. I know it feels like that right now but consider this: Rachel's cousin's daughter went to school with me. She died of cancer at seventeen. She was a beautiful girl who fought like crazy to stay alive. I remember Julie's funeral, which shook up all the kids. We never thought somebody young like us could die."

Life is so fragile. It only takes a moment . . .

Lori listened to her mother but showed no emotion.

"That was young."

She was part of a generation that had grown up with mass murderers gunning down school kids, when active shooter drills were commonplace and death images were rampant on the internet. Just a month earlier, 19 children and two teachers had been killed in a school in Texas, and she was also a secondary victim of the Highland Park murder spree.

Babs shook her head, trying to imagine her daughter's childhood.

What a sad world she'd growing up in.

Shirley decided to get things moving.

"Sit down, please. Let's figure out what's going on. I need to sit, you know. My arthritis is killing me."

She turned her chair toward Lori, stared straight at her, and smiled.

"I know what you are going through, Lori. Let's begin right there. I became pregnant at sixteen, only I didn't have a loving, supportive family. My father was an alcoholic and nearly killed me when he found out, and I thought of killing myself. Thank God I didn't. Of course, this was before Roe v. Wade, and abortion was outlawed everywhere. Luckily, my best friend's mother helped me get an illegal abortion. Against all odds, I went to college and law school and had a successful career as a woman's lawyer."

She smiled again at Lori.

"So, there's plenty of hope for you, my dear. First and foremost, abortion is legal here in Illinois. You won't have to hide or anything like that."

Babs cringed when she saw Lori's reaction to Shirley's mention of suicide.

"Your mother and I don't rally and petition for abortion. We work hard for the right to choose, for the right to be masters of our own bodies."

Lori nodded.

"You must understand, Lori, that keeping the baby will wipe out your chance to be a kid, to experience your last year of high school with proms and dances, and to fully experience college living on campus with other kids without hiding from any mean gossip. Putting the baby up for adoption will make you wonder about it for the rest of your life. Abortion eliminates these problems, and it will allow you to return to your life."

Lori met Shirley's intense stare and surprised Shirley and her mother.

"Abortion also wipes out a life!"

Her voice was shaking. Babs and Shirley exchanged concerned looks.

"Babs, please go to the kitchen and get us some coffee and some of that cinnamon coffee cake Rachel left here. Lori, go into my bedroom, please. You'll see a pair of my blue shoes and a sweater in my closet. It's time for us to take a ride."

Lori looked at her mother with a helpless expression. Babs shrugged and motioned for her to do as Shirley said. She went into the kitchen for the coffee and cake. Everything in the house was clean and uncluttered. Shirley demanded it, and Rachel conformed. Her mom had told her that Shirley was married and divorced when they had first met. Those were the days of closet gays. Now, most people felt much freer to live their best life.

Babs picked up her phone and texted Mark.

"Out with Lori. Home late. Stacy at Joanie's."

As soon as Babs and Shirley finished their coffee and cake, they ordered the car from the doorman. Shirley maneuvered herself into the front seat next to Babs, where she could give directions to somewhere near the University of Illinois.

Lori was confused.

"What are we doing here?"

Shirley smiled.

"It's our busiest clinic, Lori. When girls like you get in trouble, they come here. Help me out of the car, please."

Lori didn't move.

"I'm not ready to make a decision."

Babs spoke up.

"Honey, Shirley just wants you to see the clinic. We aren't making any decisions today."

The Planned Parenthood Clinic was nice and clean, like any other good medical clinic. The walls were painted a soft yellow, and the floor had white tiles. The lighting was neon, and it produced an electric buzz. A nurse in a white coat over blue scrubs sat behind a Formica desk.

A screen ran videos explaining the abortion procedure, adoption help, and birth control methods.

The waiting room held six young girls fiddling with their phones, watching videos, or just staring into space. Now that Indiana and Wisconsin forbid abortion care, Illinois was struggling to handle the number of patients crossing the state line.

Lori looked nervous.

"That girl sitting in the back looks like she's ready to deliver."

Shirley looked.

"In Illinois, one can get an abortion up to twenty-four weeks."

Lori shivered.

Babs thought back to her mother's story, during the early 70s, when abortion was illegal, and her mother's roommate almost died from a back-alley abortion. Now, with Lori pregnant, she understood why her mother and Shirley became so devoted to the cause.

Several people were waiting in line for various services, but Shirley had a special relationship with the people working there and she knew all of them by name. The nurse led them to an examination room. She smiled at Lori and invited her to sit down.

"The procedure only takes about ten minutes. Our doctors are very qualified. You can be back to normal in one to two days."

Lori shook her head.

"I'm not ready yet."

"That's fine. No pressure."

The nurse gave her several pamphlets, including two about abortion and one about helping those who wanted to keep their baby.

Lori couldn't handle it. She felt queasy. She left the clinic and waited in the car for Shirley and her mother. Babs appreciated Shirley's good intentions.

"Thank you, Shirley, you've been very helpful, but we're putting too much pressure on her right now."

"Babs, you can't let her keep the baby. It will ruin her life and yours, too."

"Shirley, it has to be her choice."

They helped Shirley up to her apartment and rode home in silence. Babs tried to keep quiet, but she couldn't.

"Lori, I'm sorry if Shirley was overbearing. It's your choice. When we get home, you need to tell Dad."

"I know. I'll tell Dad, but no one else, not for now, until I decide what I'm doing."

After they pulled into the garage, Lori bolted out of the car and straight to her room. Babs inhaled a garlicky aroma coming from the kitchen.

Thank God someone in our family likes to cook.

Stacy and Lassie met her halfway through the door.

"Mom, we went to see the Elvis movie. You said you have his records. Will you get them for me? I liked the film, but I hardly thought he was gorgeous. He could sing. Where are the packages? Didn't you and Lori go shopping?"

"Slow down, Stacy. I have Elvis records, but we can't play them without an old-fashioned record player. They're different than what you're used to. They're 45s and 78s."

"Dad's making chicken parmesan. Can we go buy a record player after we eat? By the way, what are 45s and 78s?"

We Won't Go Back

Babs entered the kitchen and plopped down on one of their wooden chairs. An impending summer storm quickly darkened the room. Mark turned away from the stove to look at Babs.

"That must have been one hell of a shopping trip. You look drained."

"We weren't shopping. We went to see Shirley. Lori has a problem."

By then, Lori was standing in the kitchen.

"I'm pregnant. It's my problem."

Babs jumped when she heard Lori. Mark stared and said nothing. Stacy appeared behind Lori, excited, as if she were living in a reality show.

"Wow! Are you getting an abortion? Or am I going to be an aunt? I hope it's a girl."

Lori whirled around to face her sister; fists clenched.

"Stacy, I promise I will kill you if you tell anyone, and that includes Joanie. When I make my decision, I will permit you to talk. Do you hear me?"

Stacy smirked.

"Okay. I promise. Are you and Josh getting married?"

Suddenly, thunder cracked and rumbled. It shut everyone down, especially Lassie, who hid under the table. Lori called the dog and went back upstairs, where she laid down on her bed with Lassie and the fuzzy pink elephant that Josh had won for her at the county fair. She was drained. She expected her dad to come up until she heard him tell Stacy to go watch Shark Tank, her favorite show. She knew that her parents would now go at it.

Mark cleaned up the kitchen and put the dinner he had made in the fridge for a future time. Babs stood up and approached her husband.

"Mark, we have to talk."

"About what? It seems like you and Shirley already decided for her."

"Not at all! I felt helpless when I found out. I thought Shirley could explain things easier. I'm sorry; we should have included you. No decision was made. It's Lori's decision."

Mark said nothing and went upstairs. Babs poured herself a cup of coffee and added a bit of Kahlua. As she twirled her hair in her fingers, Jill called.

"Is everything all right? Stacy just told Lin that you have a problem with Lori, but she can't tell anybody."

Babs took a deep breath.

"I'm going to kill that kid. Everything is fine. Just a possible breakup with Josh."

I know Jill doesn't believe me, but I promised.

"Babs, I'm here if you need me."

Babs barged into Stacy's room.

"Honest, Mom, I didn't tell!"

Stacy ducked the stuffed bear Babs threw at her.

Mark knocked on Lori's door. She told him to come in. He looked around at all the teenage girl things, like stuffed animals, fluffy pink rugs, and music posters. He sat on the side of the bed and held Lori's hand.

"I want you to know that we will support your decision to abort or keep the baby. You know, I was raised to believe that a baby was a human from conception, and I will help raise your child. Hell, I have two older sisters and three young brothers and your mother."

Lori interrupted him.

"Mom and Shirley said Judaism believes that the mother's welfare is more important than the fetus, and abortion is allowed. Dad, I'm so confused right now and so mad at myself."

"Since when did Shirley become religious?"

"Huh?"

"Nothing. What did Josh say?"

Lori started to cry.

"He said, 'We'll work something out,' and then he disappeared. I haven't heard from him in two days."

Mark's eyes flashed. He tried to hide his anger, but he couldn't.

"I'll kill him."

Lori sat up.

"Please, Dad, please don't talk to him. Please don't."

She squeezed her father's hand.

Mark kissed Lori.

"I love you."

He left the room before he exploded. Up until that point, he had liked Josh.

That night, the rain, thunder, and lightning didn't let up. Stacy slept like a baby, but Lori's secret kept her up all night. Mark and Babs didn't fare much better as each of them tossed and turned, worried about their family's future.

Chapter Twenty-Nine

Lori had a lot on her mind as she began another day at camp. When she was asked to work with the twos and threes, she could hardly refuse. They were adorable but a handful. She watched tired mothers drop them off and pick them up. Her grandmother had worked tirelessly to get laws passed so that women could work at jobs previously not available to them and earn equal pay as well. Now, as women spent less time at home with their children, quality daycare was more important than ever.

As Lori thought about the young mothers she observed, she wondered how she would be able to work at a job she liked and raise a child, especially without a husband or a college degree.

At three months, she felt no life yet inside her, but she knew a baby was growing. When she went to all those rallies with her mother, she was sure of her decision to fight for abortion. Now that she was so vulnerable herself, she was more than sure that a woman needed to have the right to choose, but she was not sure at all about her own situation.

Norma, one of the women she worked with, noticed something different.

"Lori, you're peeing a lot lately. Maybe the doctor should test you. Women can get bladder infections easily, but antibiotics can cure them."

Lori knew Norma meant well. It made her realize that she would soon be showing, which would prompt all sorts of unwanted questions. She would also have all kinds of the usual pregnancy problems, like concentration and fitting into her clothes. School was starting in four weeks, so she knew that she had to decide her future before it was too late. Not surprisingly, Lori was scared and confused and didn't know who she could talk to.

Babs, meanwhile, was feeling more and more like a forgotten member of the family. Everyone was doing their own thing and she felt left out. For the next week, with one less car available, Mark drove Lori to camp in the morning, and Stacy had friends pick her up for wherever she was going with them. In the evening, they ate dinner with little to no conversation. Each of them tried to avoid discussing Lori's situation and then separated into their corners for the rest of the night. Tension was building, and Babs struggled to contain herself. Finally, after too many days of pretending nothing was wrong, she exploded.

"This whole charade must stop! I've had enough of everyone acting like strangers in a boarding house. We can't solve anything like this. We must address the elephant in the room."

She twirled her hair in her fingers. As Lori attempted to get up from the table Mark put his hand on her arm.

"Sit down."

Lori looked at Stacy, who just shrugged. Babs nodded, and Lori took a deep breath. Mark cleared his throat.

"Have you decided anything?"

Lori didn't say a word.

"Have you heard from Josh?"

Lori stayed mum.

"Lori? You need to talk. Now."

"No on both."

Mark was trying to contain his frustration.

"Are you avoiding everything? Josh should be part of your decision, you know."

Lori pulled her arm away from Mark and ran upstairs, putting an end to their discussion.

As Babs twirled her hair against her head, Mark got up, grabbed his car keys and jacket, and stormed out of the house. Stacy and Babs looked at each other and said nothing. They ate the rest of their dinner in silence. Babs watched Stacy nibble on her pasta and salad. She looked scared. Her father was usually the calm one in the family who could handle everything, and he had just stormed out of the house. To Stacy, Lori was messing up their happy home. She finished eating and told her mother she was going upstairs to watch a movie on her laptop.

Babs decided to leave both of her daughters alone.

What more can I say to Lori right now? She's got to decide for herself.

An hour later, Babs heard banging on their front door. As soon as she opened it, she saw a crazed young man who immediately ran into their house.

"Josh!"

"Where is Lori? Where is she?"

Josh paced back and forth in the living room, scaring Babs a little. Stacy popped up on the landing upstairs, saw that it was Josh and immediately disappeared. Josh stormed around the room, barely able to contain himself.

"Lori! Where are you?"

Babs wasn't sure what to do. Josh's intensity frightened her.

"Josh, calm down, please."

Just then, Lori calmly walked down the stairs.

"Come with me, Lori."

Josh sounded like he was ordering an inferior officer in the army.

"We have to talk."

Before Babs could say a word, Lori and Josh had left the house. Josh drove past their high school and a half a mile away to a park, where he stopped the car. His eyes were flashing as he turned to Lori and began yelling at her.

"How dare you send your father to threaten my father! How dare you! My dad didn't know anything about us. Having sex, I mean. Fuck! Your father was a total jerk. He embarrassed my dad in front of his campaign team."

"Josh, I didn't send him! Are you kidding me? I would never do something like that."

Josh looked at her as if he didn't believe her.

"Josh, I told you about my pregnancy over a week ago, and I haven't heard from you. Not a word. Nothing! It's your baby, too!"

Josh gripped the steering wheel. His eyes blazed and his knuckles turned white.

"I told you, Lori. I told to go away and put the baby up for adoption. I also told you I would pay. So, what's the fucking problem?"

"You son of a bitch! I hate you, Josh."

Lori opened the car door and started to get out. Then, she turned around quickly and slapped Josh across his face. As she maneuvered out of the car, she slipped and fell, hitting her head on the open door.

Josh got out and rushed around to her. He pulled her away from his car.

"Lori, are you okay?"

She didn't respond. She was breathing, but unconscious. Josh called 911. He started to call his father but decided to wait on that. Instead, he called Lori's parents. By the time the paramedics arrived and loaded her onto a gurney, she was conscious and moaning. He met her parents at Glenview Hospital.

Babs was a wreck. Stacy sat in a corner, staring at her phone. Mark showed up, looking ready to punch the first person who talked back to him. No one spoke to each other as they waited for the doctor. Finally, after an agonizing half-hour, they were told that Lori was conscious and still going through tests.

Babs had to keep Mark away from Josh, who was quite upset. Mark had a hard time believing Josh's story, that Lori had fallen while getting out of the car. He thought Josh had attacked her.

The visitors' area was full of family members waiting to talk to doctors. Each one held a beeper like they were waiting for dinner instead of what could be shattering news about their loved ones. This was no place for confrontation.

Babs twirled her hair in her fingers. She was thankful for the sign that reminded people to wear masks and keep their conversations to a whisper. She took the beeper and marched Mark out of the room for a "calm down" walk. This was out of character for her. Mark was normally the one who kept *her* calm.

Time to put on your big girl pants.

Two hours later, after endless pacing and cups of coffee, her beeper went off. Babs and Mark were led into a small office with a big picture of a ski resort dominating one wall. Stacy stayed in the waiting area, glued to her phone.

Sort of out of place, but cheerier than the sterile waiting room.

Josh followed them inside, and before they could react the door opened and a green-eyed, red-haired young woman entered.

"I'm Doctor Wilson."

Josh and Mark perked up, as they both initially thought she was a nurse.

"You may all sit down. Who am I talking to?"

Babs nodded.

"We're Lori's parents and this young man is . . ."

"Her boyfriend."

As Josh extended his hand, Mark gave him a withering stare and then turned his attention to the doctor.

"How is our daughter?"

"Lori will be fine, don't worry. Sorry it took so long, but we wanted to do some additional tests. She received eight stitches to the back of her head. We conducted a series of scans, and thankfully there is no damage beyond that nasty cut and a concussion. Because of that, we need to watch her for forty-eight hours to make sure."

Babs twirled her finger in her hair. She and Mark looked at each other, still fearful but somewhat relieved. Josh stood with his mouth open, not sure how to respond. The doctor sighed and continued.

"I'm sorry to tell you the bad news, which is that Lori was twelve weeks pregnant, and the fall caused her to lose the baby.'

No one said a word, but a fly on the wall would have seen a collective wave of relief fill the room. Babs and Mark reached for each other's hand and Josh literally smiled as the doctor turned to address him.

"Since Lori's fall was an accident, I need you to come with me and complete a report. Mr. and Mrs. Wood, your daughter is in Room 323. Even though mask-wearing has become voluntary outside the hospital, we require everyone here to comply. Your daughter will be groggy because of the concussion and the stitches, not to mention the blood loss she's experienced due to her miscarriage."

Miscarriage. That terrible word sounds so welcome now.

As Dr. Wilson left the room, Mark clenched his fists and glared at Josh.

"I would like to see your police report. Are you sure you didn't assault our daughter?"

Babs grabbed her husband.

"Stop it."

Mark followed Babs to the elevator and up to floor three. She texted Stacy and told her to wait there for Jill to pick her up. As they tiptoed into the room, they saw a large bandage covering the back of Lori's head, along with a few tubes hooked up to her arm to test her vitals. Babs gulped and gripped Mark's hand.

Oh God. She looks so groggy and fragile and so thin and pale.

Mark shook his head and whispered.

"She doesn't look right, Babs. Might be something else besides a concussion."

He took off to get a nurse. As Babs stepped closer, Lori opened her eyes.

"Hi, Mom."

She smiled and shut her eyes.

Mark came back and pulled Babs out of the room.

"I forgot that the doctor said she lost a lot of blood between the head injury and the miscarriage. They're monitoring her in case she might need a blood transfusion."

"She's in good hands here, Mark. We should trust the doctors."

"I know, but I want to kill the boy who did this to her."

Babs shook her head.

"Josh didn't make her fall, Mark. Please stay away from him now. It will only make things worse, especially for Lori and her recovery."

I wonder if she knows she had a miscarriage.

Lori opened her eyes again.

"Hi, Dad."

She tried to smile.

"I'm exhausted."

She squeezed Mark's hand and closed her eyes.

He and Babs stayed another two hours, watching the nurses come and go, take blood, and check vitals. Lori tried to talk but she couldn't stay awake.

"Mark, I don't want to leave her. Only one person is allowed to stay overnight. I'll stay, and you go home with Stacy and take care of Lassie."

"Okay, I guess you're right. Call me if anything changes. Do I have to pick up Stacy?"

"Pick her up at Jill's. She keeps texting and asking about Lori. She needs family now. Give me a few minutes to get a coffee and a roll downstairs."

Babs made a hasty trip to the first floor, where she purchased a latte and a bag full of croissants. They were Lori's favorites, though she doubted she would eat much of anything.

Mark approached Lori and gave her a soft kiss.

"Rest now, Sweetheart."

Babs touched Mark's arm as he turned to go.

"Please pick up Stacy and go straight home, okay?'

She smiled at Mark as he left.

Miscarriage. Oh my God.

Chapter Thirty

Due to Covid, the hospital was short of available rooms, which meant that Lori and Babs were stuck overnight in the old wing.

Ugh. It smells like stale medicine and urine.

Babs stared at the walls of Lori's room, with its layers of cream-colored paint and no cheery pictures to raise the spirits. The only chairs were straight-backed and metal, which meant she was going to have a very uncomfortable night. To make matters worse, the nursing staff walked the halls all night, responding to moaning patients and the relentless beeping of blood pumps and heart monitors. She also heard the constant sound of ambulance sirens, reminding her that people kept entering the hospital for a variety of bad reasons.

As Babs tried to find a comfortable position to sleep, she wondered about the patient on the other side of a flimsy curtain. She saw a stuffed animal poking out from the end of the bed, but she couldn't tell if it was a little kid, snuggled up with another fuzzy friend, or perhaps a pregnant mother who had just miscarried.

I need to focus on helping Lori recover.

Fortunately, probably due to the painkillers she'd received, Lori slept through the night, despite the frequent visits from nurses to check her IV and oxygen levels.

At six a.m., Lori was awake and talkative. Babs could barely open her eyes and her head hurt from no sleep and a night of too much worrying. Lori seemed to wait until her mother was wide awake before asking the inevitable question.

"Mom, the baby?"

Babs twisted her hair through her fingers and shook her head.

"You miscarried, Honey."

Lori didn't look surprised at all.

"I thought so because I have a pad on and I'm bleeding."

She turned away as tears flowed down her face. Babs reached out to comfort her and thought better of it.

Let her be, at least for a moment.

"Mom, did Josh . . ."

"No."

Josh had left the hospital the previous evening without seeing Lori. He had no idea if she had lost the baby, and Babs was afraid to ask Lori how she felt about him.

Not yet. There will be plenty of time for that.

"No, Lori. Josh must've gone home, but he did send flowers."

Lori kept her head buried in the pillow.

Mark is right. I want to kill that boy, too.

Babs wanted to hear Lori's story about the accident. So did the police. Before she could find a way to start asking questions, an elderly woman appeared in the doorway, clad in a white coat and comfortable shoes.

"May I come in?"

Babs looked at the woman's grey hair pulled up in a bun and her warm smile. She nodded, and the woman stepped inside and pulled up a chair next to Lori's bed.

"Hi Lori, I'm Dr. Polansky. I'm a gynecologist. I need to examine you and ask you a few questions. Is this your mother? Do you want her to stay in the room, or should we ask her out?"

"She can stay."

Dr. Polansky smiled at Babs and took Lori's hand.

"Do you and Mom know that you miscarried?"

Lori nodded. Babs did, too. Dr. Polansky looked again at Lori.

"How do you feel about losing the baby?"

Lori took a deep breath and looked at Babs before answering.

"Just tell Dr. Polansky how you feel. There are no right or wrong answers right now."

Lori nodded.

"Well, I felt sad when I found out, but truthfully, I guess I was also relieved."

The doctor patted Lori's hand.

"My boyfriend, the baby's father, didn't want anything to do with the baby . . . or us. I mean, I think so. He sent flowers, but probably because his mother told him to."

Dr. Polansky got up and moved the flowers to the window.

"Let's give them some light, shall we?"

She sat down and told Lori to continue.

"Okay, at first, my dad wanted me to keep the baby, and my mother wanted me to get an abortion, but they said it was my choice. I was so confused. I hated the idea of destroying a life, but I wanted to go to college and live a normal teenager's life."

Dr. Polansky looked at Babs and turned her attention back to Lori.

"The decision was made for you, Lori, but your body is still confused. For the next two to three weeks, you may have pain, bleeding, and mood swings. You've lost blood from the miscarriage and the cut on your head, so you need to eat a good diet, take iron pills, and rest more than usual."

Lori and Babs both took a deep breath.

"The good news is that when you get older and feel ready to become a mother, you should have no problems getting pregnant. There should be no lasting issues from this miscarriage."

Babs closed her eyes, as if she were praying.

"Thank God. Thank God. Thank God.

"Mom, please step out now, and I will examine Lori.

Babs left the room and went down the hall to the bathroom. As soon as she locked the door, the tears came.

Seventeen years old! She's gone through so much for her age. Will she ever be the same?

Babs washed her face and brushed her teeth in the cramped bathroom.

She should be excited about her prom instead of recovering from a miscarriage.

As she left the bathroom and walked back toward Lori's room, a policeman stopped her.

"Excuse me, but I need your permission to talk to your daughter about the accident."

Babs signed the form and returned to the room as Dr. Polansky was leaving.

"Your daughter should be fine. Once the physical healing is complete, make sure she's being taken care of emotionally. You may want to set her up with a therapist to help her through the psychological fallout from all of this."

Babs nodded and thanked the doctor. She was happy that Mark wasn't there, especially when the policeman interviewed Lori. She absolved Josh from everything, insisting that it was all her fault.

Just moments later, a tray of breakfast food with eggs, toast, and juice was brought in for Lori. Babs sipped her coffee while Lori ate a little.

"Mom, did you and Dad want me, or was I an accident?"

Of course, we wanted you.

Babs took a moment before she answered, wanting to be as truthful as she could.

"Of course, we wanted you, Honey. You were part of our five-year plan, but you arrived early, in Year One! We knew it was God's will, so we married while I was in my last year of law school. Dad had just started a job at a real estate office and was studying for his license. Our plan was for me to work for five years and save up some money, and then we would have kids."

Babs took another sip of her coffee and laughed.

"Dad came from a big family, so he wanted a dozen. I wasn't exactly ready for that! After you were born, two sounded good to me. To be honest, Lori, if we hadn't gotten married, I probably would have had an abortion. So, thank God we got married and had you! Aunt Lizzie and Mark's sister, Ann, did a lot of babysitting. My mother was battling lung cancer at the time, and I was trying to be with her, too. She was happy to hear that a baby girl was on the way."

"Gee, Mom, you sure had problems, too."

"Honey, life always presents problems. It's how you deal with them that makes the difference. Dad and I are here to help you right now."

Later that day, Mark and Babs brought Lori home. They hoped they could all return to normal as soon as possible. Lori requested that no one outside the family be told about her pregnancy or miscarriage.

"I'll tell everyone I was in the hospital because of the accident."

Lori spent the next two weeks at home, and Babs stayed with her, refusing to join any more rallies or petition signings. She even postponed dealing with her father's estate. She knew that her priorities were now with her family. She even kept quiet while they spent two days letting Mark try to fix the air conditioner before calling a repair service.

Since Mark had a job near Max and Benny's, he often brought home deli food. One day, Babs put together a nice-sized corned beef sandwich, plus some potato salad, and brought it to Lori, who was sitting on a lounge chair with an unread book in her hand.

"Thanks, Mom, but I'm not hungry."

Babs snapped.

"Enough, Lori. It's been two weeks. I know you're still recovering, but we must talk about the elephant in the room. Josh has made no effort to contact you. It's time for you to forget him already and consider yourself lucky that you haven't ended up with someone that arrogant and selfish."

Lori looked up, alarmed. Babs rarely got so upset.

"Mom, you don't understand. I love him."

Babs twirled her hair in her fingers.

"At your age, you are infatuated, which hurts more than love. Do you know that?"

Lori shrugged.

"I hear what you're saying, Mom, but Josh is different."

"Is he? Is he, really? Lori, I went to high school, you know. Usually, getting involved with a high school sports hero adds up to nothing but disappointment and pain. This guy my girlfriend and I thought was God in high school ended up working as a two-bit magician for a party company. By the time he was twenty-five, he was going to AA meetings."

Babs picked a piece of corn beef off Lori's plate.

"When a boy like Josh is so selfish and uncaring, and he gets away with it, he will probably become a devil of a man. My mother fell in love with a guy like that, and it had lasting effects on her, my brother, and me. Lori, please find someone like your father, who cares about his family in all the right ways."

"You are talking about Papa. You and your brother hated him. I didn't."

"Yes, Papa. You're right. He was terrible to us and nice to you. For one little visit at a time. Consider yourself lucky that you found out what Josh is really like. A person shows their true colors in times of crisis. It's time to forget him now."

I just hope your father will.

"Now eat something, Lori. Call your friends and get out of the house. Show Josh that you are a better person than he is."

Babs went back into the house before she said anything more about Josh she might regret.

Lori knew her mother was right, but she still found it hard to believe that the boy she thought she loved, who had told her he loved her, too, could be so cold and mean.

Since returning home from the hospital, she had texted Josh four or five times and called and left messages. He never responded. She collected the cards, costume jewelry, and posters he had given her and threw them into the garbage. Then, she retrieved them, boxed them up, and put them in her closet. She wondered if the baby had been a boy or a girl. She remembered dreaming about marrying Josh and having a house full of kids. She still had a picture on her desk of the two of them at homecoming. They looked so handsome—Josh in a tux and Lori in a tight-fitting purple dress, with her hair up in curls.

Babs was still shaken up from her encounter with Lori.

I can't believe I said some of that stuff, but she needs to hear it.

She texted Jill.

"HELP."

They met for a short lunch at the Pancake House. The place was crowded, so they sat at a table next to a window. Babs stared at the busy shoppers hurrying by. Jill sat across from her.

"It's nice to see shoppers back on the square. For a while, after the July 4th shooting, people were uncomfortable being in Highland Park."

"Yeah. I can't stay long. I left Lori alone, and she is still pining for that jerk."

"You didn't leave her alone. I dropped off Lin, Joanie, and Stacy at your house on my way over here. If those three don't get Lori out of the house, nothing will."

We Won't Go Back

"No wonder you were late."

They burst out laughing. Jill was Babs' soulmate, and the only friend she had told about Lori's pregnancy and miscarriage.

Lori met two girlfriends at the mall. She wore a scarf over her head to hide the bald spot where she had stitches. She and her friends looked at clothes and talked about basketball, dances, and their senior year. They avoided her accident, and all seemed to go well until Lori came out of the bathroom and overheard her friends talking.

"Lori isn't right. I heard she and Josh broke up after the accident or right before. We're her best friends. Should we try to get her to talk?"

Lori left the mall without a word to her friends. She pulled out of the garage and sped home as fast as possible. She wondered how she would be able to go back to school in three weeks, or if she would hide in her bedroom and finish her last year online. She and Josh were voted to be prom king and queen.

Lori picked up her favorite stuffed animal and talked to her as she usually did when she was upset about something.

"Me and Josh? What a joke!"

Chapter Thirty-One

Even after Lori's accident settled the question of having an abortion or keeping the baby, Babs and Mark had a hard time getting over their differences on the issue and what to do about Josh. Mark favored keeping the baby, and he still wanted to confront Josh and his family. Babs was worried about Lori and wanted her to do therapy, while Mark thought that would be a waste and that the family being there for was enough.

Lori just wanted to hide.

The whole situation was creating a schism between her parents. Babs created excuses to stay up late, such as paying bills and doing laundry, so she could avoid going to bed with Mark. When she finally did go to sleep, she made sure that Lassie slept between them.

One night they finally reunited. As Babs quietly entered the dark bedroom, Mark, who was standing there in his birthday suit, grabbed her. Her heart quickened when he pulled her to him, and his tongue quickly explored her mouth. She tasted his toothpaste and smelled his Old Spice. Suddenly, their romantic encounter stopped when Mark pulled away and laughed.

"You've been eating the rugalach Lizzie brought for Lori. Your mouth is full of cinnamon and sugar."

Babs laughed, too, as they moved into bed together.

After three weeks of avoiding each other, their lovemaking triggered conversation, which they had both sorely missed. The timing was good because Lori had recovered enough by then to resume going out with her girlfriends. However, all was not back to normal. She was still picking at her food and checking her phone for a message from Josh. Stacy was tired of tiptoeing around her sister and having sleepovers at

Joanie's and Lin's, and Lassie couldn't handle another walk with Babs. They needed to be a family like they were before the accident.

We need a picker-upper after all we've been through.

A message from Babs' "new" half-brother, Byron, gave them a chance for something fun and adventurous. She was sitting at the breakfast table that Sunday while Mark made his famous pancakes when she saw a message on her phone.

"Babs, come visit before your girls go back to school."

"Really?"

"Yes! Business is slow and I can take time off. Cheers, Byron."

Babs showed Mark the message.

"Honey, my office is so busy now. Take the girls, and I'll watch the home front."

Stacy had her head in her phone, but she could sense something fun was happening.

"Mom, where are we going?"

"London! Byron invited us."

"Wow!" When? I've never been farther away than Florida."

Babs turned to Lori.

"Sounds good to Stacy. What about you?"

Lori looked up with a less than enthusiastic expression on her face.

"I guess it would be fun. I thought you were upset with your half-brother."

Babs sat down and started to check ticket availability on her iPad.

"He dropped the lawsuit and he's trying to get to know us. I'm more upset with my whole brother, who won't talk to me, as usual."

She poured herself a cup of coffee and texted Byron, Jim, and Larry.

"Girls, we have to get out of here in a week to make it back for Aunt Tillie's birthday party and the beginning of school, so cancel any appointments you might have and check out your closets. It's cooler in London than it is here.

Babs went into another gear. She twirled her hair in her fingers as she began to calculate what they had to do to get ready.

"Mark, are you sure you can't join us?"

We both know it will be better if he stays home.

For the next week, they were busy arranging the trip.

Thank God our passports are current.

They had planned a trip to Israel with the temple that had been canceled due to Covid, so they had passports for the girls. Lori had one more doctor's appointment, where she received the okay to travel. Stacy insisted on buying new clothes, while Lori, who had lost weight and needed clothes, had no interest in shopping. Babs stocked up on dog food for Lassie and people food for Mark, even though he would probably make himself all the things she hated, like ribs, liver, and crazy casseroles.

Jim texted back.

"No way."

Larry had surprised them all with first-class tickets on British Airways. Stacy and Lori had never flown in such luxury so it would be a treat for them.

Funny, every time Jim and I went with Dad to London, we flew first class.

Chapter Thirty-Two

In the middle of a busy week, Babs drove to Skokie to see her great-aunt. She had some family questions. At the Jewel food store, she picked out a bouquet of lilies to give Tillie. One could never bring food to Aunt Tillie's house. She would be insulted.

Lizzie met her at the door.

"So glad to see you, Babs. Instead of being excited about her coming birthday party, Mom's been down. Your company may help."

Aunt Tillie was standing by the window in one of her floral-patterned house dresses. Aa Babs walked over to her, Tillie pulled back the curtain and pointed.

"I'm worried about that little sparrow. She hasn't left her nest all morning. She has three babies, and she has been squeaking for her mate to take over, and he hasn't come. I hope he is still alive."

Lizzie put her arms out, as if to say "more mishigas!"

Birds? She's worried about birds?

"Aunt Tillie, maybe he sees you and doesn't want to reveal where the nest is. Sit with me. I have some questions about the family. The girls and I are going to London, and my grandmother was from there."

"You'll miss my birthday?"

Tillie sat down and stirred her glass of tea.

"Of course not. We wouldn't miss it for the world."

Babs took a bite of a poppy seed cookie.

"Gail's daughter and her family can't come to my birthday. Something with the school. She's the one who was raised in California, and family doesn't mean the same as it does to a family that grew up together in the family building. Is Jim coming? He hasn't responded."

Tillie looked sad as she took a sip of tea.

"So, Babs. What do you want to know?"

Babs put the cookie down and twisted the hair on the back of her head.

"I want to know the truth about Grandmother Bess. I never knew her or anything about her. I would love to find her family in London."

Tillie looked up.

"Sometimes, the truth hurts."

"I know. Believe me, I know."

Tillie put down her glass of tea and looked at Babs.

"Here is what I know. Pa kicked our sister Barbra out of the house for being with a non-Jew, so when our oldest brother Jake came home from the war with his blue-eyed, blond, pregnant wife, my sister Sarah and I decided to accept her as a Jewish member of the family even though she was not Jewish in any way at all. We tried, but it wasn't easy for her or us. She told us her mother was Jewish. I doubted it, as she knew very little about our religion, but we all played the game, including Pa. Jake, of course, was his oldest and favorite son. I don't know your grandmother's maiden name, but you are named after her. Maybe you could find it in your mom's papers. All I know is she came from a farm outside of London. Your mom told Lizzie that her mother was abused by her father and left as soon as she was old enough to get out. Your grandfather, my brother Jake, was crazy about her. We couldn't criticize her in front of him. She died too young from lung cancer. Jake never recovered."

Babs sat back in her chair and took a deep breath.

"You're right, Aunt Tillie. The truth can hurt. No wonder my mom worked at the abuse center."

Lizzie perked up.

"Sherrie and Shirley won a case against a prominent real estate man who abused his wife. It was all over the news back in the eighties. Your grandmother was always nice to me. She was different, more modern than the rest of us, and she had that English accent."

Tillie went to her bedroom and Lizzie offered Babs a frozen challah to take home.

"How's Lori?"

Babs twirled her hair in her fingers.

"The bandage is off, and her head is fine, though it will take a while for her hair to grow back. I think she should get a short haircut, but she's trying to keep it long."

"Mom and I are worried about her, and we are hurt that we weren't consulted."

"Lizzie, you know how I feel about you and Aunt Tillie. Lori wanted to keep it in the immediate family. This was so hard on the four of us. I'm still so worried about my daughter."

"I understand, Babs. My Aunt Dora miscarried, and she became very depressed, and she was married. Keep a watch on Lori."

Babs hugged her aunt and knocked on her great-aunt's door.

"I'm leaving, Aunt Tillie! We're looking forward to your birthday party!"

"You don't have to yell. Mom doesn't even wear a hearing aid. I do. I look more her age now than she does, with my wrinkled, spotted skin."

Babs almost bumped into a neighbor who walked in as she was leaving. Aunt Tillie always had an open door for friends and family.

As she paused on the porch, Babs remembered what her mother had told her years ago.

"If something happens in the Jewish community, Aunt Tillie will know about it."

Even Larry knows about Aunt Tillie.

Babs bet it was Jill's mother who had told Lizzie about Lori's situation. They played mahjong together.

Or maybe the rumor about Aunt Tillie being psychic is true.

Babs knew that it probably would be better if Lori's problems were out in the open, and that it's hard on the body and soul when you hide things. She kissed the mezuzah on Tillie's door as she left.

Only frozen challah. Tillie must be depressed.

Babs realized she would have to prepare dinner. She went to the Sunset grocery store, grabbed a cart, and loaded it with green vegetables, cut-up fruit, and ready-made chicken breasts. She started to check out and realized Stacy would be looking for rugelach, so she bought some cookies. When she entered her house, she stopped for a few minutes to text some friends to remind them about Tillie's party. Then, she hurried around the house to take care of all the last-minute details before leaving for London.

As she did, she wondered about what Larry had told her about Aunt Tillie.

Was she really the de facto head of Chicago's Jewish mafia?

Chapter Thirty-Three

Mark dropped off Babs and the girls at the international terminal, where they handed their luggage to a first-class porter and went straight to the British Airlines VIP lounge, where they enjoyed a buffet of British deli meat sandwiches, crushed potato salad, tomato and cheese salad, scones, and beer or tea.

Babs and Lori laughed when they checked out Stacy's heaping plate.

"Are you afraid they will starve you on the plane?"

"I'm taking pictures to send to my friends. I won't eat it all."

An hour later, they were escorted to their gate like VIPs. On the airplane, they were led to the first-class section, with separate bunks that turned down into beds with private individual screens. Soon after takeoff, they were presented with a chicken-and-rice dinner on a white linen tablecloth. Once they finished dinner, the lights went out, and they slept like babies until the lights came back on and they were served a cheese omelet and jelly scone for breakfast.

Babs, Stacy, and Lori were the first ones off the plane and the first to get their luggage. Stacy was thrilled. She'd already left the plane with British Airways earphones, towels, socks, and a toothbrush.

"From now on, I am only flying first class!"

Lori laughed.

"Good luck with Dad."

The flight attendant wished Stacy a good holiday.

"Thanks. We're on vacation until Labor Day."

Babs smiled.

"Stacy, here they talk British English with a different accent, and we talk American English with our accent, and many of the words they use here have a different meaning than in the States. It takes some getting used to. I remember my first trip. I was ten, and Jim was eight."

First-class customs with the hired porter went fast. They made sure Stacy kept quiet while they answered the required questions.

"Why are you in the United Kingdom?"

"Reason for travel?"

"Where are you staying?"

Babs twirled her hair in her fingers.

Stacy, please don't say anything.

She tended to give out too much information, but this time she was too excited to talk.

After their passports were stamped, the three of them looked for Byron, who they hardly knew and wouldn't recognize. Babs kept her cell phone handy.

A tall, thin young man approached them. His hair and mustache were sandy-colored, and he wore a tan, buttoned vest under a herringbone coat.

"Babs?"

Instead of a bear-hug, the typical American greeting, Byron shook their hands and ushered them into a yellow van while he packed their luggage in the back.

"You have a lot of luggage, Babs. Good thing I rented a van."

"What kind of car do you have?"

"A two-passenger Jaguar."

"I guess you knew a small car wouldn't work with three of us and our luggage, especially a two-seater!"

"Okay, girls, as we drive along the motorway to the city and my townhouse, please tell me what you want to see in London."

Both girls responded together.

"The Eye, and the jewels!"

"Why does everyone want to see the Eye? It is just a big, crowded rollercoaster. Lucky for you, though, I can get VIP tickets. It's the first thing we'll do tomorrow. I'll be knocking you up quite early."

Both girls clapped, but Stacy was confused, and Lori cringed.

"Knock us up?"

She whispered her response, but Babs still turned around quickly and shook her head to shush her daughter.

"That's not what he meant!"

Fortunately, Stacy chimed in.

"Byron, why will you knock us?"

"Stacy, you catch everything," Babs said. "That's British for saying, to wake you, like to knock on your door."

"That sounds better than hitting us," Stacy said. "I bet you didn't know that on our mother's side, our great grandmother was born in London."

Byron glanced at her in the rearview mirror.

"Oh! You know, on my mother's side, my grandmother lived in Chicago for a short time."

Babs perked up. "

How odd. We should explore that."

"Before you go home, I want to take you to the countryside where my mother's family lives. We can explore the story with relatives there who can recite the area's history going back hundreds of years. We will be home soon. Traffic is light right now, and we're almost there."

They soon stopped in front of rows and rows of white-columned, three-floored townhouses in the fashionable Mayfair neighborhood. Babs looked around with wonder.

"Byron, these are different than I remember. The neighborhood I remember had high-rises and modern stores. There is a park, and the buildings look old and charming. We have so much to talk about."

"Right. You see, when my mother died nine years ago, Dad, I mean, my dad, your dad, too, of course, he let me decide where I wanted to live since I was twenty-two and alone."

Did I tell the girls enough about Byron? And what about their grandfather cheating?

Byron exited the van and unloaded the luggage from the back.

"Now, just wait here while I park the auto. No chauffeurs here."

When Byron returned, Lori and Stacy helped carry the luggage up the stairs to the second floor of the townhouse while Babs took in Byron's interior-designed apartment.

This is nothing like Dad's modern mansion.

The 100-year-old Victorian building had crown moldings, painted doors, crystal chandeliers, and silk curtains. The mahogany wooden sofas had creamy white silk coverings and pillows that matched the colorful wall coverings, next to a large, marble and wood fireplace.

Byron seems talented and so lovely.

Babs smiled when she thought about how angry she had been when she first learned of his existence.

"Mom, come up to the second floor," Stacy said. "We're in the kitchen."

"Byron, are you whipping up a dinner for us?"

He placed plates of tea biscuits and pieces of white cheese on the green-dotted, black granite island counter.

"No way am I whipping up dinner! Sorry, but I don't cook. My partner does. I've just laid out some starters. There are droves of restaurants along here. What do you want to eat?"

"Fish and chips!"

Stacy and Lori didn't hesitate to announce their top wish.

Byron turned to a huffing and puffing Babs.

"There sure are a lot of steps in this place. Are you going to tell me the bedrooms are up on another flight? Because I need my purse. This was a larger townhouse than the one Dad had when I was a kid. "

"I'll get your purse, Mom," Lori said. "Sit on the patio. "The view of the park and garden is beautiful."

Byron grabbed his car keys and herringbone sport jacket.

"I'm going to get fish and chips. Be right back. There are some starters on the counter."

"Can I come?" said Stacy.

Byron nodded, and they ran down the steps and over to the garage. They slid into Byron's green Jaguar. Stacy laughed when she realized the passenger seat was on the left.

"I know the British drive on the wrong side, but I didn't realize how strange it would feel sitting up front like this."

"Excuse me, Stacy, but it's *you* who drive on the wrong side. We were driving our horse carriages on the left before you were even a country. And by the way, watch how you cross the street. Look right first."

"Okay, you win. I guess you were talking funny way before we became a country, too."

He laughed.

"Not funny, just a different English. You are as cute as a button, Stacy."

Stacy blushed.

"Can I ask you something secret?"

"Yes, of course, but I may not answer."

She took a deep breath.

"Did my Uncle Jim really punch you in the chin?"

Byron smiled. He held his hand up by his right chin.

"He caught me by surprise. I was lucky, nothing broke, but I'm still sore."

"My uncle is strange. I haven't seen him in years. He never came to my Bat Mitzvah, and he never calls my mom back."

Byron and Stacy returned with several bags of food and cardboard boxes from a fish-and-chips restaurant. Stacy explained what they had.

"We picked up all kinds of London snacks with weird names, like sticky toffee pudding, which isn't pudding, but a muffin, and then we got crisps, which are potato chips. We also have Jaffa Cakes, which are orange candies; and funny pink fudge."

Babs laughed, reached into her purse, and pulled out some dollars.

"Byron, Stacy will bankrupt you if you're not careful."

"Mom!"

"Babs, this trip is on me," Byron said.

"No, Byron, we are paying our way."

"Mom, let your father pay through his will."

"Stacy, you are right. I'll tell Larry we're sending the bills to him and to take off the cost of our trip from the estate. He's charging us for whatever he does anyway, you know. Just think what a lawsuit would have cost."

Byron opened bottles of stout and soda and held up his glass.

"Cheers."

"To jet lag!" said Babs.

Stacy raised her soda.

"To the best trip ever!"

Lori hugged Babs.

"Thanks, Mom. I really did need to get away."

Chapter Thirty-Four

The following day, Byron woke up his new jet-lagged family. Babs looked at him quizzically, as if she wasn't sure who he was or where she had been sleeping.

"Oh, Byron! It's you. I thought I was in a church. What have you done with the ceiling in this room?"

Byron looked slightly embarrassed.

"My partner is an artist, and he painted it."

Babs smiled.

"For a gay man, he certainly likes to paint women."

They both laughed.

"Will we get to meet him?"

Just keep Stacy out of this room of half-naked Victorian women.

"You won't meet my partner this time. He went on holiday."

She looked up again.

These figures are very well done.

"Byron, did our father order that ceiling? Was this his bedroom?"

"Yes, Dad did a lot of the design in this townhouse. He let me do the sitting room."

"I forgot to tell you how much I love the first floor. It's so English with the crystal chandeliers, silk sofa chairs, and gold framed pictures of the countryside. I also need to apologize. I went through racks of Dad's expensive suits and pants, never thinking you might want some. You and I, plus Jim, sorry, need to meet with Larry to check out Dad's safe deposit box. He was a lover of good jewelry."

Byron handed Lori some towels embroidered with the initials "RG."

"In this room, you'll see boxes of Ronnie's things. I couldn't give them away even though it's been three years since he's been here."

Babs laughed.

"I knew he was here. I can smell his scent on the clothes in the closet."

Byron smiled.

"Polo cologne. The scent lasts for years."

Before he left, he made sure Stacy and Lori were awake and getting ready.

"Make haste, everyone. The Eye is now one of the most visited attractions in London. Even though I have VIP passes, it will be crowded."

After being hustled out of the house with juice, coffee, and biscuits, Byron drove them down the south bank of the Thames River and into a garage across from the park. When they emerged into bright sunshine, unusual in London, Byron assured them that he had his umbrella with him just in case.

Stacy, Babs, and Lori looked up at the Eye across Westminster Bridge.

"How big is it, and how long does it take to ride?"

Byron had expected Stacy's questions, so he had read up on the Eye and he answered like an experienced guide.

"A ride on the London Eye takes thirty minutes, and it travels at a speed of less than one mile per hour. It is four hundred forty-three feet high, and it has thirty-two capsules to ride in."

Babs smiled.

"I'm impressed."

So was Lori.

"I read that a husband-and-wife team came up with the idea for a millennium Ferris wheel. It went up on March 9, 2000, missing the millennium celebration by two months. We do have VIP passes, right?"

Stacy stopped.

"Look! These squirrels are red. We only have gray and black squirrels back home."

Byron stopped to look at the two red squirrels scrambling along with the crowd of people.

"Stacy, that is very unusual. Most squirrels here are gray or black, too. I've never seen a red one, yet here are two of them."

Lori gave her mother a knowing smile.

"There goes Stacy, entirely off the subject at hand."

As they walked closer to the Eye, it appeared larger and higher than in the pictures they'd seen. Stacy, in her cutout jeans, skipped along the grass. Suddenly, she stopped and turned towards Byron.

"Has anyone ever fallen off?"

Byron smirked.

"It is only a Ferris wheel, and it is very safe, checked continuously, and you are in sealed pods, not out in the open."

They still felt apprehensive as they entered one of the pods.

At the top, the 360-degree view was spectacular. One time was enough for Lori and Babs, while Stacy convinced Byron to take her again.

"You are wearing me out, Stacy. I'm more than twice your age."

"Stacy laughed.

"You're closer to my age than my mother, who's your half-sister. How did that happen?"

"My mother had me when she was forty-two. I was an accident."

"I think I was an accident, too."

The Ferris wheel swung to a stop. Their pod swayed back and forth. Stacy grabbed onto Byron while several other tourists also gasped nervously. He held her for a few seconds until all was back to normal.

Later that day, Stacy confessed to Lori.

"I'm in love with Byron."

Lori rolled her eyes.

"He's your half-uncle, silly, sixteen years older than you, and you're way too young to think you are in love with anybody."

Lori stopped talking as soon as she realized she sounded like their mother. Then, hearing her own words, she smiled, knowing she was having fun without thinking about Josh or the baby. When she noticed a couple with a baby in an enormous navy-blue English tram, she looked, but she didn't give it any extra thought.

"Plus, he's gay."

Stacy sulked for a moment and smiled at her sister.

So far, the weather was holding up, so they stopped at Gail's Bakery, which was within walking distance. They sat outside at a cute, black metal table with a colorful umbrella. Byron had eggs, Lori ordered a cheese sandwich, Stacy asked for one of their famous sticky rolls, and Babs had a jelly scone with a cup of Gail's favorite white coffee. They had fun picking out baked goods to take home. Babs let the girls deal with the pastries while she admired the beautiful English garden across the street. Besides the petunias, four o'clocks, and hollyhocks, a family of ducks swam in a meandering stream. She felt so peaceful.

Thank God Jim and Mark stayed home. It would never have been so loose and easy.

Byron gathered the girls and sat them down.

"Tomorrow, we will do some heavy touring. The Tower and the castle, and the museums. It's still early afternoon. What would you like to do now?"

While the three talked, Babs raised her hand.

"I would love to go to Portobello Market. My mother used to talk about going there on her honeymoon with my father. *Our* father. She met Sophia, one of her mother's cousins, who told her some disturbing stories about her mother."

"Portobello is just a few miles from Chelsea. We can go there today. Funny, my mother and grandmother were named Sophia, which is a common name here, and they both loved that market. I remember going there for something called cheesy pasta."

"My mother talked about pasta with an odd cheese she ate in London. Maybe our families had more in common than Ronnie."

"In three days, we will go to the country and talk to my family clan," said Byron. "My Uncle Albert is only five years younger than your Aunt Tillie and he knows our family history going back years. I would love to come to your aunt's birthday party. I need to travel to the States to settle some things with Larry. How lovely it would be to do both at once."

"Byron, that would be grand."

Stacy laughed.

"Grand? Really, Mom, are you British now?"

They found their van and headed onto the motorway toward the market in Chelsea. As they drove, Byron put on his tour guide hat again.

"The Portobello Market began in the nineteenth century. It was on one of the most famous streets in the world. The brightly decorated stalls and red, blue, yellow, and white buildings stretched for over a mile. It started as a produce market, then an antique market, but it soon developed into an outlet for every type of collectible and a variety of merchandise."

It still was one of the significant antique high-class flea markets in all of Europe, like Chicago's Maxwell Street Market back in its heyday. There were no Vienna hot dogs, but it offered the delicious smells of ethnic food from carts, just like in Chicago's old market. Antiques in the States were out of fashion, but not in England. So many shops still had enormous carved cabinets, highly polished mahogany tables, decorative plates, marble statues, and trinkets from the past. Babs bought one of those tea servers with stacked colorful English plates. She wasn't sure how she would get it home.

The crowds were huge, but calm and organized. It was hard to stay together, as each person in their party had a different interest. They planned to meet at the Jewish deli in two hours. Byron took charge of Stacy. After about 50 minutes, they ran into each other by a group of incredibly talented street musicians. Babs had purchased a colorful bowl she hoped Byron would like for his kitchen. Lori bought some beautiful, embroidered tops, and Stacy selected fudge. They joined the large crowd while two men in black caps and Beatle-style tailored suits, along with a woman in a paisley-colored dress, played tunes like *Hey Jude* and *I Want To Hold Your Hand*. Soon, the audience was singing along.

Afterward, they tried to find the place with cheesy pasta that Byron's mother and Babs' mother had loved, but no one knew what they were talking about.

Stacy ran toward a colorful red and yellow booth with cages holding cats. A big sign above the booth said RSPCA, which was England's main dog and cat rescue. She sat down on the cement next to a cage holding a salmon-colored cat.

We Won't Go Back

"Would you like to see her out of the cage?" the lady said. "She is sweet and would love to be in a home with older children. She is a special cat, you know, a polydactyl, which means she has extra toes."

The cat purred and settled into Stacy's arms.

"Mom, can we take her home?"

Babs laughed.

"No, we live in the States, silly."

Stacy wasn't about to take no for an answer.

"Byron, you can adopt her."

She looked up at him, pleading.

"I have a cat, dear Stacy. My neighbor is watching her. I wasn't sure if she would bother you. Dad hated cats."

All three of them stared at Byron and Babs made her pitch.

"We love all animals, Byron. We have a collie now, called Lassie. Our cat, Velveeta, died five years ago. Come on now, brother. Let's go home and rescue your cat. What's her name?"

Stacy returned the cat she was holding to the rescue woman.

"Thank you. That was interesting about her toes. If I lived here, I would take her home."

"My cat doesn't have any extra toes," said Byron, "but she is a sweetie, though she is getting old and not that active and would find another cat too intrusive. She had a friend who died three years ago. We call my cat Plum. My mother had a plum pie sitting on the table, and as a kitten, she jumped on it, so we started to call her Plum."

They gathered their shopping bags and walked toward the van.

"Home or the deli?"

The deli won three to one. Stacy was the only dissenting vote, as she was full of fudge and pastries, and her mind was fixated on cats.

"You should have voted with me," she said. "Who ever heard of a Jewish deli putting corned beef on bagels instead of rye bread, and not having rugelach?"

They laughed.

Finally, back at home after a long, full day, Babs and Byron happily went to their bedrooms to enjoy a nap while Stacy and Lori set out for the townhouse three doors down the street to rescue Plum.

They ran up the three steps and knocked on the door. A curly-haired, green-eyed young man in a Polo shirt and blue jeans opened the door. He had broad shoulders and was tall, maybe six feet. Lori stood and stared while Stacy wasted no time explaining why they were there.

"We belong to Byron down the street, and we've come to rescue Plum."

A dimpled smile spread across the young man's face.

"You must be Byron's American family. I'm happy to keep watching Plum. She and my grandma's cat are friends."

Stacy shrugged.

"Okay, but I want to take her to Byron's place. I love cats and dogs."

"Come in then while I get her for you."

They walked into the first floor sitting room. It was a typical, English-looking room furnished in 50s style with a flowered seat-cover on the sofa and chairs, dark wooden cabinets covered with embroidered dresser scarfs, and windows covered by lace curtains.

Stacy whispered to Lori, who was smoothing down her hair.

"What is wrong with you? You aren't talking, and you look scared."

"Oh, Stacy, he's gorgeous!"

"Jesus Lori, you better not get into trouble again."

"Shoo, Stacy. Just be quiet and don't mess up stuff for me."

We Won't Go Back

The young man came down the steps with an elderly, gray-haired, woman, plus a meowing grey tabby cat in a cage. His bespeckled grandmother shook both girls' hands.

"Come in and sit down. I'm Claire, and this is my grandson, Alan. We love Byron and his partner. Byron was so worried about your trip. Has everything gone well so far? Can we get you a pot of tea?"

Stacy shook her head.

"No, thank you. We rode on the Eye today and went to a market. I would like to take Plum home now, please."

Alan turned to Lori.

"Can you stay a while? I'm eighteen. How old are you?"

"Seventeen."

Lori surprised herself with her answer, as she had been feeling like she had aged tremendously over the past few months. She felt relieved to remember that she was still so young. She sat down on the sofa while Stacy grabbed the cage with Plum.

Claire smiled as she watched her grandson look at this nice young American.

"Lori, why don't you stay and visit with Alan. He is bored with his old grandmother and could use some young blood to talk to."

Lori and Alan blushed.

"Stacy, are you okay going back on your own?"

"I'm fourteen now."

Stacy stood up, took the cage, and walked out. As she did, Lori texted her mom to be on the lookout for her.

"I'll be back later. Don't worry about me."

Chapter Thirty-Five

Babs greeted Stacy and the cat at the front door to Byron's place. She was glad to see her youngest becoming independent but concerned about her oldest growing up too fast.

"Look at you, Stacy. What's with your sister?"

"She stayed to talk to this guy who she thinks is gorgeous. I told her to stay out of trouble. I think Byron is better looking."

Byron burst out laughing, spilling his beer as he placed it on the table.

"I think Alan is gorgeous, too, but he is only eighteen and straight, so I must stay away from him. But your sister is just the right age and she's straight."

Hmm. It's really that simple, isn't it?

Stacy opened the cage and busied herself chasing Plum, but Babs was interested to know more about Alan. She looked up from her coffee and scone.

"So, who is this boy? This young man. Sorry."

"My neighbor's grandson, Alan, is from Bath and he will start college at Oxford next week. He's been visiting his grandmother for about a month. She lost her husband six months ago and she's lonely. He is a stunner and a good kid."

Babs smiled.

"That could be a godsend. Lori's boyfriend broke up with her after almost two years, and she's been depressed."

Babs gave Stacy a look and signaled her to say no more. Stacy opened the refrigerator and took a piece of corned beef from her leftover sandwich. She tried to lure Plum to her, but it didn't work.

"Stacy, cats don't like corned beef, not even Jewish cats."

"How do you know, Mom?"

"Just a hunch."

Byron went into the kitchen and came back with a catnip treat, which he handed to Stacy.

"I can tell you are dog people. Try this. Cats are not attracted to people's food except tuna, and they come only when they are ready."

Stacy rolled her eyes and smiled at Byron.

The catnip worked wonders. Plum and Stacy quickly became friends. After watching an English comedy show on the television, she went to bed with Plum, and Byron went on his own.

Babs stretched out on the comfy cream and green sofa, opened a book, and waited for Lori. It didn't take long for her to doze off with the book open on her chest. About an hour later, she jumped up when Lori quietly knocked on the door. She turned on the light, opened the door, and in walked a slow-moving, dreamy looking young girl, one Babs hadn't seen in quite a while.

My daughter is back.

Babs smiled.

"Okay, my dear. Tell me."

"Mom, Alan is gorgeous and so nice. I think tonight was the first time I didn't think about Josh."

Babs smiled.

"Thanks for the trip, Mom."

She kissed Babs and walked slowly up the stairs.

Oh my gosh, she's smitten.

Babs took a deep breath and sat down long enough to send a text to Mark, who was still worried about Lori and steaming with anger toward Josh's family. After all, the two families had known each other for years and Mark felt that Josh's parents, his father in particular, had been terribly irresponsible with their son.

As Babs got ready for bed, she reflected on how much Josh had hurt Lori and the sad results of unwanted teen pregnancies.

Somehow, I'm not so sure this is all over.

Chapter Thirty-Six

Byron's wake-up calls came early in the morning. He greeted everyone with his upbeat demeanor and positive attitude.

"This is your London guide, my lovelies. On today's schedule, we will be taking in the Tower, the Crown Jewels, and the changing of the guard. Breakfast in twenty minutes."

Babs opened her bedroom door.

"We are girls. Make it forty."

After a quick breakfast of cheese, salami, biscuits, and scones, they took off in their big yellow van. Lori and Stacy got busy on their phones, texting their friends back home so they would have London "news" when they woke up. Babs turned her attention to Byron.

"Tell me about your mother. When did she meet Ronnie?"

"His firm had an office in London, and I think he came out for a week every few months. He hired my mom to take care of the townhouse and to be a secretary when he was in town, and to be a, how do I say it, a guide for visiting guests. Ron and my mom were sexually involved, but not romantically. My mother was carefree and fun. She had been married very young and then divorced, and she wanted to be independent."

"That is how I remember your mother, fun and carefree and very pretty. My mother was afraid of Dad, and she made us afraid of him, too."

Byron shrugged.

"Sorry to hear that, Babs, but not my mother. She wasn't afraid to talk back to Ron and she would laugh when he started giving orders. Perhaps it was fortunate that he was gone most of the time. We were taken care of and free to follow our own pursuits."

"Byron, do you miss him? Our dad. I still have so much anger inside me, based on my youth and the divorce, so I love him, and I hate him. This is terrible to say, but my best years with Dad were the last three, when he became sick and dependent on me."

Byron nodded.

"I was always jealous of you and Jim, but I seemed to have had a better relationship with him. It was long distance and infrequent, but good. I regret that I never saw Dad the last three years when he was so ill."

"Had you told me who you were, I would have let you see him."

Byron smirked.

"I'm sure you would have!"

He looked back at Lori and Stacy.

"Young ladies, put your toys away. We are almost there. Here is your guide's lecture: The Crown Jewels are in the Waterloo Branch, a medieval fortress on Thames River. Besides housing the jewels, the Tower was a prison for many years. It housed Anne Boleyn, one of King Henry the Eighth's wives."

They had a special pass for parking and to enter the building ahead of the lines. As they exited their yellow van, the girls sang "We all live in a yellow submarine," all the way down to the Waterloo Branch, where the jewels had been kept since 1303. They walked along the cobblestone pathway to the Tower.

Stacy skipped along, trying to keep up with Byron's pace.

"I know something you haven't told us. The jewels were hidden in Canada during World War II so the Germans couldn't get them."

"Interesting," said Byron. "It means we thought we might not win the war. I'm glad they are back in London."

In the Tower, he stopped in front of several cases.

"How would you like to wear that solid gold crown with its 440 precious stones? There are over 100 pieces adorned with thousands of diamonds, pearls, emeralds, and other precious stones. Did you know that Queen Elizabeth wore the crown at her inauguration in 1953?"

After staring a while at the jewels, Byron suggested they look at the armor display. The girls told him to look at it and come back for them.

"What would you like to do? I'm guessing I should take the museum off my list."

"Byron, we want to go shopping," said Lori.

He smiled.

"Of course, you do, and the dollar is strong. How about Harrods? I'm sure you've heard of it."

Walking through the largest and most expensive department store in Europe was like touring a museum. Unfortunately, VIP passes weren't available, so they could not get into the famous tearoom, the chocolate shop, and some other departments. They walked around admiring without buying, something most tourists did. Finally, they gave up and walked a mile to Selfridges Department Store. The girls found clothes and souvenirs at reasonable prices.

Once they were back in the van, Byron had a plan.

"It is time to see how the locals live."

Dinner was in an English pub called The Goat, situated near Byron's townhouse. It was an ancient white building, resembling a cottage, with low ceilings, wooden beams, and a log fireplace. The tables had lit candles, and the lanterns above were authentic but wired with electricity. Byron was well-known to the owners and regulars and seemed quite in his element. There seemed to be many more men than women in the establishment. Many of them came over and shook the girls' hands.

"My family from the States," Byron said. "Fix them up with the best."

That was his way of introducing them.

He sat Babs and the girls down on heavy, dark wooden chairs next to a long, thick wooden table. Soon, bottles of ale, cider, plates of meat, roast potatoes, Yorkshire pudding, and steak and ale pie were passed around.

This is almost like being at Aunt Tillie's house.

"Eat some more," Byron said. "You hardly touched the plate. So, how does our grub compare to that in the States?"

One patron volunteered to teach Lori how to play darts.

"From the States? So how do you Yankees like the mother country?"

Stacy started to answer but Babs cut her off, which made everyone laugh.

By the time they left, they were all stuffed and happy. Fortunately, they were close to home, which was good because Byron was a tiny bit high. He went right to sleep when they arrived, and Babs, a little tipsy, too, was ready to lie down as well.

Those men kept filling up my glass.

Lori had been offered ale, but she drank soda with Stacy. Babs planned to text Mark and then read her book, but she went to bed before she could do either one. Stacy played with Plum, and Lori walked down the road to see Alan. She pulled out some biscuits from one of her shopping bags to give to his grandmother.

Three hours later, Lori knocked on her mom's door.

"Mom, are you up?"

"Of course."

Babs jumped up and opened the door for her daughter.

"Is everything all right?"

Lori sat down on the bed.

"Being with Alan for the past two days made me realize how selfish and immature Josh has been. Alan is so sweet and considerate. He lets me talk, and he values my views. He knows that abortion in the United Kingdom is legal for the first six months, and that there are clinics everywhere. From our conversation, it seems that women have more rights here in England."

Babs twirled her hair in her fingers.

"Did you talk about your experience?"

"Not everything. Just my accident, and stuff about campaigning against the Supreme Court's ruling against abortion and the rallies for women's rights. We talked about how we need a woman as President."

"You're right, Lori. Go for it."

Lori laughed.

"Anyway, Alan is leaving tomorrow. We promised to stay in touch, but we're too far away from each other for anything to happen."

Babs hugged her daughter.

"I'm so glad you've learned that you can like another boy. Think about it. You and Josh started dating when you were only a year older than Stacy."

Lori sighed.

"When you put it like that, we were so young and naïve."

Lori grabbed her purse and said good night to her mom.

She's growing up so fast!

"Don't write Alan off quite yet, Lori. London isn't that far, you know, and you now have family here."

Lori threw her mom a kiss and quietly tiptoed to her room.

Chapter Thirty-Seven

Byron knocked on all the doors with what had become his morning ritual.

"Forty minutes. Prepare for a long day. We are going to the country after the changing of the guard. The weather is cooling down. Bring a jacket."

"You sound like my mom with all the orders."

Stacy lifted Plum off her leg, but the cat wasn't ready to leave the warmth of the blue feather comforter.

"Plum, wait right here while I take a shower."

She happily made it to the third-floor bathroom before Lori. As she heard the door open and close, Babs rolled over and remembered what Byron had just said. It was cloudy, but that was typical weather in London.

Sounds like blue jeans and a long sleeve top.

Lori felt sluggish. She had stayed up late, texting her girlfriends about Alan. It had been a month since she heard from Josh, which probably meant he had a new girlfriend, at least according to one of her friends. They all agreed that he had turned out to be a jerk, but Lori had still not told them everything. She had told Alan about the accident but not her pregnancy. Although he was very sympathetic, Lori wondered how he would feel about the miscarriage or her having an abortion. Would he still want to see her? What about the boys at her school?

Babs went down to the kitchen to help Byron get breakfast ready. She made Mark's blueberry pancakes, and Byron made the tea and coffee and prepared yesterday's muffins.

We're leaving in two days. I need to get something for him.

"Byron, you've been an unbelievable host, and I'm so happy we connected. I'll try my best to get Jim to talk with you at Aunt Tillie's party."

Byron smiled and kissed her on the cheek.

"My sister!"

An hour later, they were on their way to Buckingham Palace to the changing of the guards. It started at 11 a.m., but they had to arrive there early enough to get close. The Queen's New Guard, in their bearskin hats and red tunic outfits, were led by a regimental band from Wellington Barracks. They replaced the old guard at the forecourt of Buckingham Palace. The guards there are not allowed to smile or talk to anyone. The ceremony took about 45 minutes, and for the contingent from Chicago, it was awe-inspiring. Stacy was excited.

"Will we see the Queen?"

Byron shook his head.

"No, my dear, I'm sorry to say, but Her Highness spends the summer in Scotland at her Balmoral Castle. She is ninety-six years old, you know, and she's slowing down. Prince Charles, the future King, has taken over several of her duties."

Stacy frowned.

"I'm not too crazy about him."

Byron laughed.

"Join the club."

"Tell us more about the royal family."

"Well, Buckingham Palace has been the London residence of the royals since 1837. That's where they host all their state affairs and visiting dignitaries. There are seven hundred seventy-three rooms and a magnificent garden. When you see the Queen meeting dignitaries, she is always doing so here in this palace."

"Do you like the Queen?" Lori said.

"We love her! She is the only monarch most of us have ever known. She has been on the throne for seventy years. We hope she lives to a hundred so we can have a big party."

"Like Aunt Tillie," Stacy said. "She's made it to that age, but her party isn't until we get home. Can we tour the palace?"

Byron clapped his hands and signaled for everyone to go.

"Okay, mates, we are off again. We have tickets to tour Windsor Castle."

"Byron, if we are going far, I need a toilet," said Lori.

"Me too," Stacy said.

Byron looked around.

"There must be a loo somewhere close."

Babs shrugged.

"Aha, down there, near the end of the park. Good idea. Windsor Castle is only about 25 miles away, but it could take an hour due to all the traffic. Lots of tourists, like you!"

Windsor Castle, 1,000 years old, had Gothic-style buildings with enormous chandeliers and paintings from artists like Leonardo da Vinci and Peter Paul Rubens.

There's gold everywhere.

They were allowed to tour the public staterooms, which had been remodeled to accommodate Queen Elizabeth when she interviewed public figures. Queen Mary's doll house, with its complete library and elaborate furniture, was another highlight they could tour.

Lori took Byron's arm.

"Next time you come to Chicago, we'll take you to see the Colleen Moore Doll House at the Museum of Science and Industry. I think it's even nicer than this one."

Byron smiled.

"Then, I definitely must see it."

After the staterooms and the doll house, they walked around part of the 13,000 acres. They stopped to tour St. George's Chapel, with its high painted ceilings, stained glass windows, and gargoyle-type figurines.

Byron played tour guide again.

"Henry The Eighth is buried here, and so is Prince Philip, the Queen's late husband. When the Queen dies, she will be buried here, too, after much pomp and ceremony. But it is getting late, and I promised my family that I would bring you to the country to visit, so let's find our chariot."

Chapter Thirty-Eight

Byron decided to skip the expressway and drive along a series of country roads to give his family a taste of the charms of English farm country. In that setting, the animals had the right of way and they had to stop a few times to let a herd of cows pass by. The rolling green hills they observed, with sheep and cows, traditional thatched roof cottages, and ancient pubs and churches, provided a picture of a different England. The aromas of clover and wet grass filled the van with fresh, earthy odors. The drive was quiet except for the sounds of sheep's bleating, flies buzzing and Stacy complaining about a lack of cell phone service.

"Ugh! What is going on here? And it smells like you-know-what."

Babs laughed as she took photos and tried to text Mark. Lori noticed that her mother hadn't said much at all during the drive.

"Mom, are you okay? You've been quiet."

"Oh, I'm fine. I've been trying to reach Dad all night and this morning, too, but there's been no answer at all. Weird."

"Forget it," Byron said. "You'll never get a connection out here."

"Okay, but I should have been able to connect in London."

"Mom!" said Stacy. "Dad and Lassie might be golfing."

Babs laughed and twisted her hair in her fingers.

This is not like Mark at all to not be reachable.

Byron's family farm, about 50 miles outside London, now consisted of 100 acres instead of the 350 it originally had before the family was forced to sell considerable chunks to keep what they could. Along with losing acreage, the family had also shrunk down to the 11 members who currently lived there. All of them were over 60, except for Darlene and her six-month-old baby. Darlene took Stacy and Lori on a massive green truck to tour the working part of the farm, while Byron took Babs to see Albert, the 96-year-old family patriarch.

Uncle Albert was sitting on a big old wooden rocking chair with a yellow pipe in his mouth. The smoke smelled sweet, like burnt sugar. He wore a plaid shirt over baggy brown pants. His long gray hair sticking out of his cap made Babs think of the Beatles. If she hadn't been told his age, she would have never guessed it.

"Albert loves to say he is three days older than the Queen, and he heard her speak at an army base back in the war."

The farmhouse looked nothing like what Babs had imagined.

Never seen one like this back home.

The building was made from stone, covered by greenery, with arched roofs and long vertical windows dating back to the 1700s. It was situated on the highest point of the property. The smell of freshly cut grass, hay, and ripe fruit was strong, and the sounds of cows, sheep, and chickens could be heard everywhere.

Byron told Babs that up until his generation the family was poor, getting by with outdoor plumbing and growing their own food. About 50 years earlier, living in the country had become fashionable, and the area became a tourist attraction. Byron's family sold off half of the farm and updated the house. They kept the charming front edifice and added on a large modern living area. The property was lush with green fields, peaceful and serene. The sweet scent of ripe fruit and freshly cut grass was everywhere.

Byron's great uncle motioned him to come close.

"Lad, what brings you here?"

Byron smiled and whispered to Babs.

"He is trying to place me in the family."

"Uncle, I'm Byron, Sophia's son."

Uncle Albert shook his head.

"She died too young. All that smoking!"

He re-lit his pipe and looked at Babs.

"Bess's daughter?"

Babs nearly fell over.

How could he know?

Byron brought her a chair and a glass of water. Babs breathed deep and took a drink.

"Uncle Albert, why did you say that? Did you know my grandmother, Bess? All I know about her is that she lived on a farm outside of London, met my grandfather during the war, and he brought her to Chicago."

"You look just like my cousin, Bess. The same green eyes. Your face and your pretty, wavy hair remind me of her. Well, your hair is more blond. Her hair was originally black."

"My grandmother was a blonde."

Albert coughed and blew his nose. Byron gave him some tissues.

"When Cousin Bess and Cousin Sophia left here, they dyed their hair blonde, bought some fancy clothes, and went after the soldiers. I'll just say, I don't know where they got the money. Byron, get us some stout."

"Just water for me," Babs said.

She twirled her hair and pressed her lips together.

"My mother told me that my grandmother's father abused her."

"I can't tell you about that one," Albert said. "He drank too much. That's for sure. All I know is that both Bess and Sophia went to the States. They were best friends, besides being cousins. Sophia returned unmarried with two children, a daughter also named Sophia, and Charles. I never heard a word from Bess. What are you doing here? Do you fancy Byron?"

Babs and Byron laughed.

"He's great," said Babs, "but we're family."

"Yes, Bess's daughter," Albert said.

"I'm Bess's granddaughter."

She sat back in the chair.

Bess's granddaughter, Uncle Albert. I can't believe it.

Albert took a drink of his stout and slapped his leg.

"Lad, where the hell did you find Bess's granddaughter? Go get Emma."

A heavy woman in a printed housedress with long gray hair holding a dish towel came out with Byron.

"Old man, what do you want?"

She shouted at him, which to Babs was not common among the typically calm English. "We have company here, dear father, and I'm busy working on supper."

"Byron, get her a chair," said Albert.

Emma looked like she had no time to listen to her father. She shook her head and pinched her lips together before sitting on the broken-down lawn chair next to Albert, who paid no attention to her anger.

Byron shifted his head back and forth, looking from one to another. He had a smile on his face when he turned to Babs.

"My Uncle Albert and his daughter, Emma, have been putting on this show for as long as I can remember. She was twelve when her mother died. Emma helped raise her five siblings and their kids."

Albert ignored her and proceeded to explain.

"Three cousins born in the 1920s were the family leaders. They were older than the other cousins by at least seven years. In our late teens, the war took over. I entered the Air Force, and Bess and Sophia left the farm to entertain the troops. Bess and Sophia found Americans to take them to Chicago. Bess stayed, but Sophia left her American man and returned with two children. Byron is the first Sophia's grandchild, and the second Sophia's son. Two Sofias. It's confusing. Babs is Bess's grandchild, and . . ."

Emma jumped up and cut off her father.

"I'm busy getting supper ready. They are family, that is all you have to say."

She hugged Babs and grabbed Stacy, who was running toward them, while two black and white border collies followed her.

"Mom, come with me," Stacy said. "You have to see the sheep, horses, and chickens, and then you can pick apples with us."

Babs ran up the hill with Stacy. She felt happy and sad. Her mother, Sherrie, had tried to find her mother Bess's family, with no luck. Before the divorce, Babs' father had hired a detective to help. Knowing him, she bet he found joy when he found her mother's family and never told her about the connection. The coincidence was too much to believe! The first Sophia's daughter, Sophia, worked for Babs' father! Babs could believe that Byron was an accident, as Sophia and Ron were almost too old to have children.

For the next two hours, Babs and her girls met their new English family. They hugged, shook hands, exchanged text numbers, toured the farm, sat along the long wooden table, and ate fruits, vegetables, and chicken, all grown on the farm. They smiled a lot while both sides tried to understand the conversation in what should have been their common language. They were introduced to family names they immediately forgot.

The drive back to London was quiet, especially when Byron voiced his concern.

"Mates, I need to concentrate. Please keep the blather down. This is a dense, drizzly fog."

Stacy screamed, and Byron slammed on the brakes.

"There's a ghost in the road!"

We Won't Go Back

As she slid under the seat, Byron checked outside. He discovered a lost sheep crossing the road. He re-entered the van and looked in the back seat at Stacy.

"Thanks, mate. We could have hit it."

Stacy stayed on the van floor for the rest of the ride. Lori laughed.

"You've read one too many horror stories."

The next morning, they packed for the trip home. After Babs texted Mark's brother, Mark finally answered. She was relieved, but anxious.

"See you at the airport."

Something is not right.

She twisted her hair in her fingers.

Babs had worried about leaving Mark while he was so angry, but she and the girls needed a trip like this after her father's death and Lori's accident.

What happened to Mark?

In the afternoon, Lori spent a few hours visiting Alan while Stacy played with Plum, leaving Byron and Babs to make a list of all the things they needed to do when they got back to reality. Babs wanted to be sure to remember to send gifts to Byron and Albert, get the girls into school, prepare Aunt Tillie's party, and so whatever was needed for the many rallies and petitions she would help organize.

I need to figure out what is happening with Mark.

Babs twisted her hair in her fingers.

I take my husband for granted too much.

Babs went to sleep that night with a lot on her mind.

Early the next morning, she walked into the girls' room to ensure they were up. She found clothes scattered all over Lori's bed.

"What's going on? I thought we were all packed."

"She's looking for a stuffed animal from Josh," Stacy said. "I'm going for breakfast."

Babs looked at Lori, who burst into tears.

"Mom, I want to stay here. I can't go back to school as Josh's ex-girlfriend."

Babs hugged her daughter.

"I understand, but you can't stay here. Let's deal with it when we get home."

They had fallen in love with London in just a short week, cherishing the many sights they had visited and their new relationship with Byron. After many hugs, thanks, and promises to keep in touch, Babs and the girls entered the airport.

Chapter Thirty-Nine

The trip home was comfortable and uneventful. Stacy was upset because she couldn't text on the plane, but she enjoyed the food. Lori stayed busy reading a book Alan had given her. Babs, buoyed by memories of their great vacation, tried to sleep, but she was worried about problems that awaited her at home.

Something must be wrong with Mark!

When they arrived at O'Hare, Mark was there to pick them up, but he was quiet and much more reserved than usual. On the ride home, Stacy rattled on about the trip while Lori stared out the window. Babs tried to converse with Mark, but he was largely unresponsive.

What is going on?

As all three of their phones beeped with messages that hadn't gone through before, Babs tried to focus on her texts and refrained from pressing Mark in front of the girls.

Lassie was happy and jumped all over Stacy and sniffed carefully.

"She can smell fish 'n chips," said Lori.

"She missed me the most," Stacy said.

Babs twisted her hair in her fingers and tried to stay calm.

Once they were home, Lori headed upstairs with her suitcase.

"Hey, Stacy. Lassie smells Plum."

Stacy pouted.

"No, it's too long. She missed me the most, you know."

She headed upstairs with her luggage, and Lassie followed. Babs put her suitcase down in the hallway, hung up her coat, and turned to Mark, who was just standing there.

"Okay, Mark. What is going on?"

He could barely look at her as he handed Babs a three-day-old local newspaper. His picture was on the front page with the following caption.

"LOCAL MAN ARRESTED FOR HECKLING!"

Oh my God. This is why he didn't respond?

The article went on to describe how Mark had been heckling Representative Sloan at one of his recent political rallies.

Babs sat down at the kitchen table and looked at Mark.

"I'm not reading any more of it right now. Tell me what this is all about."

He stared at Babs. It took him a minute to begin.

"I went to school with Sloan. He was an asshole then and still is. He had a rally to get votes. Josh was there. When he was praised for his good deeds and his stand against abortion, I went nuts and yelled things I shouldn't have. I guess I took it too far."

Babs rolled her eyes.

"I guess you did."

"Babs, ever since the accident, I thought Lori was protecting Josh. I believed that he pushed her out of the car to hurt her, you know, to cause a miscarriage or worse. When he didn't contact her to see how she was doing, that was an act of a coward. I don't care if he's still a teenager. That's not right, and his father is complicit."

"So, what happened?"

"I spent a day in jail, made the papers, and have an upcoming court date."

"Court? You're serious? You have to go to court for heckling?"

"Harassment. Disturbing the peace. Public threats."

Lori stepped into the kitchen after overhearing the end of the conversation.

"Dad, how could you? Missy just sent me the article. I'm going to kill myself."

She ran up the stairs and Babs followed her into her bedroom, where Lori threw herself on the bed, crying.

"I can't go back to school. No way. Please don't make me."

Babs called her friend Karen, who was a social worker. She agreed to see them right away, so Babs stormed out of the house, dragging Lori with her.

"Sorry I grabbed you. I'm not mad at you, Lori. Let's just get some help."

I'd like to strangle your father right now, though, that's for sure.

Karen spent an hour with Lori. Then, she talked to Babs alone.

"I don't want to scare you, but I would keep a close watch on Lori right now. There is an epidemic of teen suicide and depression. A young girl from the North Shore just threw herself in front of a freight train. The internet and bullying are contributing to a lot of it."

Babs' eyes opened wide.

"Lori?"

She twirled her hair in her fingers.

"There is no evidence of any suicidal tendencies with Lori, but she is disturbed. The pregnancy, the accident, and the breakup with her boyfriend are a lot for a seventeen-year-old to handle. If she wants to go to a different school, we can find a private one, like the Latin School. We don't have a lot of time. School starts in a few days."

Babs was numb. After such a great trip to London, she couldn't believe everything had turned bad so quickly.

"Did Lori make another appointment to see you?"

"She agreed to see me in three days,"

Karen got up and walked Babs to the door.

"I hope she keeps the appointment."

Babs looked through her purse for a check.

"What do I owe you?"

"Nothing for today. If she becomes an official patient, it will be $100 an hour. How was your trip?"

"Great. Until now."

When they got back in the car, Babs asked Lori if talking to Karen had been helpful.

"I think so. She said I could attend a private school for my last year and still graduate from Lake Forest."

"That is a choice you can make. Think about it. Meet with your girlfriends. It's Sunday, so you can take my car. This jet lag is getting to me."

Mark and Stacy were gone when they returned. Lori went into her room and shut the door. Babs barely made it to her bed. She passed out on top of the blankets, with her clothes on.

Around four in the morning, she woke up with tears in her eyes.

Lori. Oh my God. Suicide?

She realized she was hungry, so she changed into a nightgown and went downstairs, opened the refrigerator, and took out some cheese and crackers. As she began to eat, Babs heard her name whispered, and looked around cautiously before she spotted Mark in the kitchen doorway. She fell into his arms, sobbing. He held her for a while before they sat at the kitchen table and talked.

They acknowledged that they needed to work together. The accident had solved the abortion question, but there were still lingering questions and plenty of pain to go around.

The next week was full for Babs with catching up on bills, laundry, phone calls and friends. Stacy worked on getting her mom to take her shopping for high school, and Lori went to therapy and saw her two best friends for lunch at the mall.

We Won't Go Back

"Dinner!"

Lassie was the first one to make it to the table. Mark came in from the yard, sweaty and dirty.

"Hungry!"

"Still working on the tractor?"

"Yes."

He walked into the restroom to clean up. Stacy sauntered down the steps, phone in hand, with pods in her ears.

"Where is Lori? The car is in the garage."

"Here I am."

The voice was familiar but the figure in the doorway looked foreign. Babs, Mark, and Stacy were in shock.

"Where is your freaking hair?" Stacy said.

The girl that stood before them was a pixie-cut strawberry blond in gold sandals, black sunglasses, and a short, tight gold print dress.

"My therapist and I decided I needed a new attitude and a new look."

Lori smiled nervously.

"I love it," Babs said.

"I miss your long hair," Stacy said. "You look too different, though, like a movie star."

Mark whistled.

Babs twirled her hair in her fingers.

Now, we really should watch out for how she's doing.

"I've decided to drop out of basketball and join the book club, and I'm going to work with Mom and Shirley on women's issues."

Babs was surprised.

"Are you sure?"

"Yeah. I never enjoyed basketball anyway."

Babs smiled.

"Honey, I think these are great ideas. I love your new look. Have you shown it to any of your girlfriends?"

At least her hair isn't blue or green, and she didn't decide to be a boy, or a bunny.

"Let's eat," Stacy said.

She walked out to the grill to get food.

"Missy went with me," Lori said.

She tossed a hot dog on her plate, and a piece of another one to Lassie.

"Okay, enjoy your dinner, everybody, and remember that Aunt Tillie's birthday party is in three days.

Chapter Forty

Mark grabbed his sportscoat and Lori held the corsage they had bought for Aunt Tillie. About ten minutes later, Babs glanced out the window and realized there was a problem.

"Mark, where are you going?"

"To Max and Benny's Deli."

"I told you the party was changed to the temple in Skokie. More than a hundred people are coming, and there was no room to park and eat at Max and Benny's."

"I don't remember you telling me it was changed."

"Just turn around and take the expressway, please. I don't want to be late."

Stacy grinned at her sister. They both thought Mom forgot to tell Dad.

The parking lot at the temple was almost full. People stood around the main attraction—a large blue and silver coach bus, the kind used for tourist trips.

Lori and Stacy stayed with their father while Babs looked around. They were a little shy around so many new people, especially young children, whom they had never met. Family had gathered from as far away as Taiwan and Australia. Byron and Jim weren't coming, and Mark figured it was probably because they wanted to stay away from each other.

Babs found Lizzie by the coach. She looked irritated, her face was knotted, and she was tapping her foot.

"Where is Aunt Tillie?"

"The party is catered, right?" Lizzie said. "She agreed to it. So, what do you think she did? My mother stayed up all night cooking and baking. Mom is now inside the temple, telling the caterers what to do with her food and where to put her pictures. She will probably fall asleep halfway through her party."

Babs laughed, even though she knew Lizzie was upset.

"Lizzie, this is what your mother does. You think she's going to suddenly change? Making food for everyone has been her main job most of her life. It's her mission!"

Lizzie rolled her eyes.

"Here they come."

Yale and Aunt Tillie walked out of the temple. Babs realized Lizzie might be a little jealous of her brother, who did little to care for Tillie, yet he often took center stage with his mother whenever he was around.

First born son syndrome, here we go.

Yale, dressed in a pinstriped suit with a blue-patterned tie, looked dapper. He strolled along, holding his mother's arm. Aunt Tillie was in a gray silk dress with a cameo pin on the left side. The one-half-carat diamond studs she always wore had been cleaned, and they sparkled as the sunlight caught them just right. Missing was the usual bun on top of her head. Her silver-gray hair had been cut and styled, and she wore one of her many charm bracelets on her wrist.

Aunt Tillie stood in front of the bus and addressed everyone gathered there in a strong and confident voice.

"Thank you to everyone joining me here in my celebration of being on this Earth for one hundred years. Never did I think I would make it to this age. The sad part is that many of my family and friends are not here because they weren't as lucky as I've been to live so long. My one request for this party was to show all of you the family building in South Shore. I want to thank my son Yale for making this possible. For those of you who are not joining us on the bus, I understand, and look forward to seeing you later at my party."

Yale stopped his mother.

"Mom, we have to go. You will be able to talk all day."

He took the microphone.

"Time to get on the bus. I want everyone to know that we will have a police car with two policemen and several city officials joining us at the Museum of Science and Industry."

Forty people congratulated Tillie with hugs and congratulations as they stepped up onto the bus. The rest would be at the temple in three hours to help continue the celebration. Yale did an excellent job. The blue-and-silver coach had plush seats, air conditioning, a toilet in the back, and an audio system. Yale brought a cooler filled with water, pop, and his mother's snacks: home-baked cookies and cakes. The smell of fresh baked goods filled the air, and the passengers stopped to take them from the open cooler. The crunch of cookies was heard as friends and family found seats. Most, especially the out-of-towners, were dressed in sports jackets, dresses, and jewelry—too nice for a trip to what had become a rundown, tough neighborhood.

When Yale and Tillie boarded the bus, its engine rumbled, and the air conditioning started to cool everyone inside. The music from the speakers took over the first part of the ride. Tillie leaned back in her front seat, closed her eyes, and relaxed. She planned to talk after they passed downtown Chicago.

Most of her contemporaries were gone. Only one friend in her age group was with them. Cousins and siblings had died years ago, but somehow more than 100 friends and family were helping her celebrate.

Her three children were still alive, but they had lost two grandchildren. Now, she could count six great-grandchildren and one great-great-grandchild. Unfortunately, most lived across the continent and around the world. She had difficulty recognizing the grand and great-grandchildren who had come to the party from far away.

Babs watched it all unfold.

How different today is from when Aunt Tillie and her children grew up.

Yale, instead of sitting in a belted seat, walking up and down the aisle and greeted everyone.

He should run for office.

Tillie turned to Lizzie.

"If I fall asleep, wake me when we get to the lake."

Lizzie smiled. The passengers conversed freely. Some, like Lizzie's granddaughter, Bella, who lived in Taiwan, hadn't seen each other in years. Babs talked to everyone while her family stuck with each other. Even Stacy was shy with so many unknown family members.

Lizzie shook her mother as the bus passed the downtown area and drove along Lake Michigan. The lake was calm. Temperatures were in the sixties, warm for Labor Day. Bikers and walkers were taking advantage of it. In Chicago, the snow could come at any time.

Yale turned off music and gave Tillie the microphone. She took a drink of Pepsi and began to address everyone again.

"My friends and family, thank you again for joining me on this journey. For those of you who didn't grow up by the lake, maybe most of you, you missed the glory of Chicago—the beach in the summer, the water bouncing off the rocks, the cool breezes, and the boats. Right now, we are in Hyde Park near the museum. Yale, Gail, and Lizzie went to Hyde Park High School, not far from here. The world-renowned Museum of Science and Industry was one of our favorite places to visit. The girls loved the doll house and the exhibit our dentist put in."

Babs laughed.

Even the dentist gets credit today. He must've been Jewish.

The coach stopped. A policeman and an alderman stepped onto the bus. They congratulated Tillie, talked to Yale, and disembarked. Yale announced that the museum bathrooms would be available to anyone who needed them as soon as they disembarked.

Babs watched Stacy and Lori as they made sure they had their phones.

Maybe they'll learn something nice today about our family history.

Chapter Forty-One

Fifteen minutes later, the bus took off behind the police car. Tillie took the microphone and started to talk. Her heartbeat increased as they passed so many the familiar places from her days on the South Side of Chicago: the museum, La Rabida Children's Hospital, and Jackson Park Golf Course.

Yale took the microphone from his mom.

"We used to hunt for lost golf balls and resell them, and we parked by La Rabida on Saturday nights to watch the submarine races! Does anyone else remember them?"

There was laughter from a few of his fellow relatives and friends in their seventies.

Stacy turned to Lori.

"How could they see submarines on the lake?"

"Keep quiet. I'll explain later."

Stacy went up front and took two cookies and a Pepsi out of the cooler. Aunt Tillie stopped her and smiled.

"Thanks for coming, my darling."

"Happy Birthday, Aunt Tillie. Where are the rugalach?"

Tillie pulled Stacy close to her.

"They are with the party food. Don't tell anyone. I will save some for you to take home. Go sit."

Yale gave the microphone back to Tillie, who asked the driver to stop at 71st Street before going to the apartment building.

Tillie looked out the window and smiled. She was home. To every South Sider, Jeffery Boulevard meant home. It was the main street in the area running from 67th to 95th. If one ever met someone who spelled his name "Jeffery," one knew he was from the South Side of

Chicago and had lived somewhere near Jeffery Boulevard. She asked the driver to stop at 71st and Jeffery so everyone could get out of the bus, but the police decided to keep everyone inside the coach.

Tillie stood up and leaned against Lizzie. Tears came to her eyes.

"My friends, nothing here is the same except for the railroad tracks going down the center of the street. They used to be wooden planks and the seats were made of straw, but we dressed to the nines when we rode on the IC for the half hour it took to reach downtown Chicago."

Lizzie grinned.

"As a teenager, I once caught my heel in a plank and barely missed the train. I spent the day walking with a broken heel. Mom, why didn't you buy me new shoes downtown?"

"Too expensive, and I knew the shoemaker could fix it."

Tillie took the microphone back and continued.

"This corner was once the major shopping area with two theaters, restaurants, clothing stores, bakeries, drugstores, doctors' offices, and a bank. On the opposite corner was The Peter Pan Restaurant, and across the tracks, The Jeffery Theater. Most of the women couldn't drive. We used shopping carts, or the stores delivered."

Some businesses remained, but the streets were nearly empty at 11 a.m. on a Monday morning. Those who were around paid no attention. Police cars were common in South Shore.

Mark was taking it all in and turned to Babs.

"South Shore looks much better than its reputation. There are still some stores, and the buildings are in pretty good shape."

"Mark, it's the drug wars and indiscriminate shootings that make it so tough here. A five-month-old girl was shot last month. Look at the scattered fragments of abandoned buildings and the 'For Sale' signs."

Only a few people on the party bus had lived in South Shore. The younger group was getting edgy. Yale asked his mother to let them go on to the family building.

The coach followed the police car across 71st Street, where they turned left and proceeded past O'Keefe School and onto 68th and Merrill Avenue. They stopped in front of the family building and allowed everyone to leave the bus. The street was quiet. A few people looked out of their windows, and two women and a small boy came out of the building. The alderman had informed them about the visitors.

He asked Tillie what she thought. She stared at the red brick building.

"So many memories. We should have stayed. We lived here for almost thirty years. Those were the happiest times of my life because our family lived together. One brother's family on the first floor, another brother's family on the third floor, my family on the second, and a father and sister across the street."

The alderman nodded.

"It looks the same," Tillie said. "The tree is much taller, and a few buildings are gone. The main thing missing is the feeling of safety and unity we used to have. If a child got into trouble, his parents knew before he came home. Neighbors watched out for each other. We had our own village."

Tears fell down her cheeks. She turned to the alderman.

"Why can't you do something to help the people living here? Why so many guns, and why are they so easy to get?"

A photographer from a local newspaper took her picture.

"I'm donating my birthday gifts to help the children in South Shore. We are starting a program where people can donate. Yale, please explain it to the newspaperman."

The alderman shifted uneasily. He brought one of the women standing by the building door forward to see Tillie.

"This is Ruby. If you would like, this nice occupant of the second floor will let you see the inside of her apartment, but only you."

Tillie went into her old building with the woman who lived on the second floor. She walked up the stairs slowly, thankful she didn't have to go to the third floor, where she had lived for more than 30 years.

Tillie stopped after entering the apartment.

"I was told most apartments were broken up and made into two or three."

"Not in this building. I pay $1,000 monthly for myself, my mother, and my four children. I work at the school a block away, so I save on transportation."

Tillie smiled.

"Yes, all the family kids appreciated having their school only a block away. Could I sit down? I am winded."

Ruby took Tillie into the kitchen and brought her a glass of water.

"Girl, are you really one hundred?"

Tillie took a drink and nodded.

"The kitchen was my room. I spent most of my days here. Funny, it looks so small compared to my memory of it. Are you afraid living here in South Shore, or does it just have a bad reputation?"

Ruby shrugged.

"This is still a beautiful neighborhood. We have the lake, the South Shore Cultural Center, beaches and parks, and restaurants. Most of the population are hardworking people trying to care for their families. Unfortunately, drugs and gangs are taking over, and we are losing our children. Do you want to look around?"

Tillie got up and walked around the apartment. Ruby followed behind her, apologizing for the mess her four kids made. The bedrooms and bathroom seemed smaller than Tillie remembered, and the front room larger. The walls were pale white instead of the flowered wallpaper she used to have when she lived in the building. The burning smell of cigars lingered in her mind as she remembered Hymie and his smoking. She stayed in the kitchen, remembering the days she spent cooking for everyone. The fancy new electric appliances her brother Jake bought for his English wife were still there, only now they didn't look so fancy.

Cooking for the family was sacred for Tillie. She imagined her family sitting at the lion-pawed dining room table and stopped a minute to remember the voices and sounds of those who were gone. She wondered why she had outlived her five siblings.

As Tillie walked to the back door, she turned toward Ruby.

"I would like to see the backyard where I hung all the laundry and talked with the neighbors. I haven't been back here for so many years. Thank you for making it happen."

Ruby helped her walk down the stairs.

"Mrs. Paul, please wait here a moment. I want to go back and get my phone."

As Tillie waited for Ruby to come back, she slowly wandered away from the stairs, curious to see what the backyard looked like now. She was in a wistful mood, full of bittersweet memories from days long ago.

Chapter Forty-Two

Back on the bus, the visitors were restless. They had consumed all the cookies, drank all the beverages, and talked to each other more than enough.

Yale approached the policeman waiting by the front door.

"My mother has been gone too long. Can you please check on her?"

The second policeman left the bus and went into the building. He found Ruby on her way to the back door.

"Where is the old woman?"

"I left her at the bottom of the steps. I went back to get my phone."

"Why did you leave her alone?"

They hurried down the back steps. When they reached the bottom, Tillie wasn't there. They opened the door and looked in the yard. No Tillie. They ran into an empty yard.

"Tillie? Tillie!"

They heard four gunshots, followed by a racing motor.

Backup were immediately called, pistols came out, and the policeman ran into the alley. They saw a white Honda with its windows shattered by four bullet holes. Inside, slumped over the steering wheel, was a teenager. Dead.

The police were frantic.

"Tillie, Tillie!"

They heard a weak voice coming from behind a closed garage. By then, half the visitors from the bus were in the backyard.

"Over here."

A policeman found Tillie standing still against the door.

"Are you hurt?"

He gently walked her away from the garage.

"I'm fine, Officer. Just in shock."

As soon as Lizzie saw her mother, she screamed.

"She's bleeding! Call an ambulance."

Tillie was bleeding from her right hip.

The stench of gunfire filled the air as friends and family staggered around in shock. They were all stunned, and some were crying. Photographers who felt like they had been assigned to cover a benign puff piece came alive when they realized they were now first on the scene with action pictures of breaking news.

Two ambulances arrived within minutes. They were too late to save the boy in the car, but they were a welcome sight for everyone else. Paramedics put Tillie on a stretcher, and the police moved everyone back so that rescue workers could bring Tillie to the ambulance and gently lift her inside. Her beautiful new gray silk dress had blood all over it from a bullet, which had grazed her thigh. The paramedics stopped the bleeding and treated her as best they could before they departed to the hospital.

The news broke all over the internet, radio, and television. Tillie was a celebrity before the ambulance even reached the University of Chicago Hospital's emergency room.

Breaking News:

Another Shooting in Chicago
100-year-old Grandmother Shot in South Shore. Teen Dead
Drive-by Shooting Wounds 100-year-old Celebrating Her Birthday
South Shore Shooting Kills Teen and Wounds Centennial Grandma
Tillie Paul, 100, Fights For Her Life After Shooting

We Won't Go Back

Tillie Paul Shot While Celebrating 100th Birthday in Landmark Chicago Neighborhood

Police rushed Lizzie, Gail, Yale, and Babs to the hospital while the bus, with 40 confused and worried family members and friends, drove back to Skokie.

In the emergency room, the doctor asked Tillie what happened.

"Oh my God, I lived through the Mafia days. At least they only hit their victim and no one else. Kids nowadays need shooting lessons. I'm lucky the gang member who shot me only hit my leg."

The doctor nodded and shook his head. He'd treated too many gang members over the past several years. Tillie patted his arm.

"It hurts to realize what has happened to my South Shore. When I lived there, all the mothers cared for everyone's children, and no one got hurt. We disciplined the neighborhood kids. Nobody used guns. They were for the police and the cowboys in the movies."

Unfortunately, Tillie's comments were heard by members of the media. The evening news framed her words with a searing headline:

"One-hundred-year-old former South Shore resident suggests gang members get marksmanship training to kill more efficiently."

Tillie had no idea about the backlash she was receiving in cyberspace. Her comments did not come across as she had intended, and disrespectful responses were posted all over the internet. But there were many messages of support for Tillie and admiration for her chutzpah.

Yale got up from a waiting room chair and turned off the television.

"I can't watch any more news about Mom. I never realized how distorted they could be until today. Why did I listen to her and take her to South Shore?"

Lizzie walked over to him.

"Yale, it wasn't your fault. You made Mom's dream come true. She was so happy. She'll be okay. It's a flesh wound. Mom is tough. It could happen anywhere. Remember, there was a killer in Highland Park two months ago."

Babs twirled her hair in her fingers. She had never seen Yale so distraught. Tillie's daughter, Gail, from California, sat by Babs and hung her head.

"I feel so guilty. I haven't seen Mom in two years. And now this"

Babs checked her phone and saw a message from Mark.

"How is Tillie? I'm sure she will be fine."

"Think so."

"Anyone who can comment about training gang members to shoot better is tough."

"Oy."

"I'm still laughing, Babs. We are off the bus. No one is sure what to do. The girls and I will drive down and pick you up."

"Thanks, honey."

"Love you."

Babs smiled and walked over to the coffee machine. As she poured herself a cup of coffee, a young man approached her.

"What happened with the hundred-year-old lady? Did she get shot? Is she going to live?"

Babs took a minute to answer.

"Who are you? Press is not allowed here. Please leave us alone."

He smirked and left. Babs sipped at the coffee and sat down near Gail.

About an hour later, a doctor came into the room and led them into a small office.

"First, Tillie will be fine. She wasn't even shot. We gave her eight stitches on her thigh and a tetanus shot. We think she ripped her skin on one of the broken wooden panels of the garage door. She is anxious and slightly confused, so I gave her a sedative. Her blood pressure is high, and I plan to keep her for a day or two for observation. Even though she doesn't act like someone as old as she is, Tillie is fragile. We will let you know when you can see her. Officer McDonald and social worker Bernice Hatfield want to talk to the family."

The uniformed officer had a holstered gun at his side. He carried a pad of paper, and his face was stern. The social worker, a young blonde, wore a bright-colored pantsuit and smiled as she began the conversation.

"I'm Bernice. Your mother is wonderful. Hard to believe she is one hundred years old. She told me her life history. What a memory."

Yale stood up to face the officer.

"First of all, please tell us what happened."

Lizzie motioned for him to wait. She walked to the desk and asked for a pen and paper. She returned and sat down, ready to take notes.

"Speak slowly, officer."

"Tillie told us she heard a noise and walked back toward the alley. She heard a car racing, then gunshots. She was frightened, so she dropped down by the garage door and stayed there as quiet as she could until I found her. We have identified the dead teen. He was a fifteen-year-old gang member who lived across the alley."

Officer McDonald nodded at Lizzie.

"We'll give you a written report. Anyway, the kid was either trying to hide in the car or steal it. The car belongs to a man on the third floor of the building. He took it out of the garage, went back up to get something, and decided to wait until we were away from the building. The teen got in the car, and somebody started shooting."

When the policeman started to leave, Babs stopped him.

"Officer, who are the shooters, and can Tillie have protection until they are caught?"

Lizzie looked up from her writing.

"Good question, Babs."

The police officer shifted uneasily.

Babs twisted her hair in her fingers.

"They haven't been apprehended yet. Talk to the alderman about protection. He's here in the hospital."

The officer left. They had almost forgotten about the social worker, Bernice, who stopped them from following him out the door.

"I have some good news," she said. "Mrs. Paul was so upset about missing her party that we have decided to give you our conference room to continue it. It can hold about forty or fifty people. We will have it cleaned, so it will be open for you in an hour."

"When can we see Mom?" said Lizzie.

"Now. Mrs. Paul is in Room 526. Do you want the conference room?"

"Yes, yes, thank you," Yale said. "Thank you so much."

Oh my God, now everyone will come to the hospital for a party? I guess you do crazy things for people who turn 100. And why not?

Chapter Forty-Three

When they arrived at Tillie's room, they found a few reporters hanging around. Babs told them to come back later when they would have special news for them.

Tillie looked frail and tired, but she was sitting up in bed, watching television. A tray of half-eaten salmon, salad, and potatoes was by her bed. She smiled when her children and Babs entered the room. She was busy hugging each of them when the alderman walked into the room and approached her.

"Mr. Alderman, did the young boy by the car make it?"

"No, he did not. He was only fifteen. His aunt said that once the kids in the neighborhood join a gang, they can't leave. He tried. She lost a son, too, a twenty-two-year-old."

Tillie shifted her position to alleviate any pressure on her stitches.

"Why are kids killing other kids? I'm famous for a day, you know. How can I help change South Shore? Can we raise money for a Boys and Girls Club?"

They all turned when they hear a booming voice from the door.

"I'll make sure it is advertised and promoted."

The nurse tried to remove the man at the door.

"You are not allowed in Mrs. Paul's room."

A big smile spread across the alderman's face. He turned to the nurse.

"Let Joel stay."

He turned to Tillie.

"If you agree, we can start a GoFundMe for you, and Joel can promote it. He is the face of Channel 11 News."

"What fund?" Tillie asked.

She was ignored while the alderman and the journalist planned how to promote her idea, and the nurse left the room upset about the rules that had been ignored.

Yale found the doctor and asked her about the hospital party the social worker had suggested. The doctor scratched her head.

"As her doctor, I have to say it will be too much. As her new friend, I say go for it. She is a hundred years old! It can't be postponed for long. Have family and friends come for cake and coffee for no more than an hour."

"Thank you," Yale said.

He sat down in the waiting room and made his party calls. Family and close friends were invited. Those from out of town were asked to join on Zoom. The bus did a turnaround and left from Skokie with about twenty passengers.

"What are you doing?" said Lizzie.

"The doctor okayed a small party for one hour only. I need to find the alderman."

Lizzie turned around and headed back to Tillie's room.

"I need my phone. Someone must pick up the food Mom made and the pictures she put together. Gail, please help me. Babs, would you talk to the hospital staff to see what we need to do in the room?"

Yale stopped at the nurses' station.

"Have you seen the alderman?"

A nurse looked up.

"He was talking to the deceased boy's family. Now, he is in your mother's room."

Babs started to enter the elevator when she heard a familiar voice. "Mom!"

Stacy ran toward Babs with Lori and Mark not far behind.

"Perfect timing," Babs said. "We are going to have Tillie's party in the hospital, and you can help me set up the room."

She led them into the elevator. Mark shook his head.

"Your family never ceases to amaze me."

"That's because we *are* amazing!"

For the next hour, they worked with three staff members to transform the conference room. They put up chairs and tables and Mark and Stacy ran to the neighborhood Target for decorations and tablecloths.

When they answered a knock on the door, in walked a blue-jeaned young man and an older woman with flowers and vases. They were from the florist who had been hired to provide flowers for the original party. The bouquets were beautiful mixtures of pink, blue, and yellow. The leaves were long and feathery. Their colors and fragrance made the room bright and welcoming, and the medicated, sterile hospital odor was soon gone.

The conference room didn't have a kitchen, but the hospital cafeteria made room for the food people brought in and delivered from the temple.

"Mom," said Lori. "In the hospital, everyone must wear a mask. We need to send a group message, so the guests know that medical facilities still require masks."

Lizzie's daughter took an Uber to Skokie to retrieve the purple print dress that Tillie instructed her to bring. Under the guidance of her granddaughters, she turned into the party girl she wanted to be for such a special occasion. She was tired and wounded, but ready to celebrate. They fixed her white hair in a fashionable knot and applied makeup to match the purple dress.

When Tillie and her daughters wheeled her into the makeshift party room, cameras flashed, and the guests stood up and clapped. Tillie was brought in front of an enormous white buttercream birthday cake with pink and blue flowers, which read "Happy 100 Tillie!"

Tears ran down her face.

"Thank you. Thank you."

The alderman walked toward Tillie. He was with a tall African American gentleman in a gray silk suit, whose hair was completely white. The alderman smiled and turned toward Tillie.

"We are pleased you are doing well, Tillie. I'd like you and everyone else to know that the teenage boys who did the shooting have been apprehended and will be punished."

"How is the family of the boy who was shot?" she said. "I want some of the money we collect to go to them."

The alderman smiled.

"I's sure that can be arranged. We will talk to you about it another time."

He brought forward the gentleman who had come in with him.

"Tillie, this is Don Brown. He owns a large grocery chain."

Brown stood tall and confident. He turned toward Tillie and shook her hand.

"Tillie, I am so impressed with how you have handled everything today, considering your age and your devotion to South Shore. I am proud to announce to you and everyone else that I am reopening one of our South Shore stores that has been closed for several years. And I pledge to double the money collected in your GoFundMe account."

After much applause, a microphone was put in front of Tillie.

"First of all, Mr. Brown, I want you to know that my family ran a small grocery store on 71st Street from 1946 to 1970. Every neighborhood needs a grocery store. Thank you. Next, everyone please start donating to . . . whatever it is you call our donation campaign."

"GoFundMe!"

"Mom," said Yale. "We need you to cut the cake."

Babs smiled.

Is it kosher?

Everyone sang Happy Birthday as Tillie, with Yale's help, blew out the candles and cut the first piece. Tillie tasted the white cake with its strawberry filling. Cameras flashed. She leaned toward Yale.

"Where are my rugelach and kugels and challahs?"

"Mom, they are on the food table over there."

Yale pointed to a large table with a paper cloth, covered with paper plates, plastic silverware, and food trays.

"Where are the beautiful plates we picked out with the caterer?" Tillie said. "Where is the rabbi?"

"Mom," said Lizzie, "we are in the hospital. We had to cancel the party at the temple and make a small one here with whatever we could buy."

Tillie looked up from her wheelchair and nodded. Guests surrounded her to offer congratulate and then partook of the makeshift sandwiches, Tillie's food, and the cake. Tillie ate very little. She was slowly running out of energy. After another half hour, a nurse came in to check on Tillie. After taking her blood pressure and vitals, the nurse suggested Tillie return to the room where she could interact on Zoom.

Lizzie and Yale stayed at the hospital with their mother. A bus took the stranded guests back to the temple parking lot. Some, like Babs' family, had their own cars at the hospital.

On the way home, Babs commented on Aunt Tillie's favorite saying: "Man plans, and God laughs."

A day later, Yale, Lizzie, Mr. Brown, and the alderman stood in Tillie's hospital room before a few television cameras to announce that close to a million dollars had been raised from the GoFundMe campaign. With Mr. Brown's matching funds, they had two million dollars to start programs in South Shore to help young children find alternatives to gang life.

Tillie went home, but the injury and party excitement had taken their toll on her. She kept going, but never at the same pace. Her fund continued, too. Programs and scholarships were made available to boys and girls living in South Shore. Unfortunately, the violence there continued, but the programs Tillie's ordeal had funded became a bright spot.

Chapter Forty-Four

Lori, with the help of her girlfriends, decided to go back to her regular high school. She spent a day in the beauty shop to tone down her platinum blond hair. After a prolonged debate in front of her mirror, she settled on a short black skirt, a tight pink top, and matching pink vinyl boots.

Babs drove her to school and picked her up at the end of the day. It was one of those Chicago weather specials, when the sun shined for a minute before the clouds covered the sky, and the wind scattered leaves off the trees. Babs felt the changing weather was a metaphor for whether Lori would come out miserable or happy. She sat nervously in the high school parking lot, waiting for Lori, twisting her hair in her fingers.

Please let her come out smiling.

When Lori and her girlfriends came out the front door, they were all laughing. Lori waved goodbye to them and slid inside the car next to Babs. The scent of hairspray and perfume filled the car.

"How did it go?"

Babs was nervous as she drove away.

"Mom, I was a celebrity because of Aunt Tillie. Everyone saw it on TV! That's all everyone talked about, even my teachers. They wanted to know about the party and how she was doing. Several teachers donated to the fund, and Mr. Grant told us he was raised in South Shore, not far from Michele Obama."

"You can tell him President Obama called Tillie and congratulated her."

"Get out. No way."

"Yes way. He did! He really did! He also invited her to his library opening when it's finally finished."

"That's so cool," Lori said. "Can we go, too?"

"Let's hope so."

They drove on in silence as Lori checked her phone and Babs waited for the right moment to ask the inevitable. She twisted her hair in her fingers and fired away.

"Josh?"

"We passed each other in the hall and didn't say a word. Honestly, Mom, I felt a twinge of emotion, but I also felt sorry for him . . . and angry at myself for basing my life on such a loser. His buddies were nice to me. Also, I quit basketball. Again. I never liked it. Josh wanted me to play. I joined the online newspaper, too. Mom, I think it's going to be a good year."

When they pulled into the garage Stacy attacked them before they could enter the house.

"Joanie and I made the high school cheerleading squad! I need money for uniforms."

Babs hugged her.

"Congratulations."

Lassie jumped all over them, his tail wagging, as if he could sense the family was happy and healthy again. He was right. Mark told them that he would face no legal repercussions resulting from his harassment of Josh's father. The complaint had been dropped. Babs also had good news to share. Larry had texted her to say that none of the publicity resulting from Lori's accident, Mark's behavior, or Tillie's misadventure would impact the inheritance Babs would receive, which was contingent on the names "Green" and "Greenspan" being kept scandal-free. According to Larry, since none of them had that last name, everything was fine.

Thank God for small details.

Shirley sent a text that they needed to rally before the election. Byron texted he would be in town with Alan for the winter holidays. Tillie's GoFundMe dollars continued to make a difference in South Shore. The stock market went up and down and back up again.

Babs smiled as she remembered one of her favorite slogans.

" 'We won't go back' to the way things were, but life goes on, and maybe we're going forward to better things."

She started to twirl her hair in her fingers, but this time she let if fall and skipped into the kitchen to enjoy a cup of coffee. She lifted it into the air as if she were toasting herself.

Here's to better and better . . .

About the Author

Native Chicagoan Charlene Wexler is a graduate of the University of Illinois. She has worked as a teacher, dental office manager, and as a wife, mom, and grandmother.

In retirement, her lifelong passion for writing has led to her creation of several essays, short stories, and novels. Among her books are: *Lori, Murder on Skid Row, Elephants in the Room, Murder Across The Ocean, Milk and Oranges,* and *Farewell to South Shore.* Charlene was a 2024 *Senior Illinoisans Hall of Fame* Inductee.

Coming Soon!

CHARLENE WEXLER

MILK AND ORANGES
Laughter and Tears
Book 3

In *Milk and Oranges*, Wexler's fiction and essays are grouped in five categories. **How's Your Love Life**? features two fiction pieces that will cause female readers to nod their heads in agreement, and a warm essay on Wexler's feelings for her husband, Sam. **The Cruel Club** features both essays and fiction on the tragedy of the death of a child. In **Family and Friends**, you'll meet some of the fun characters in Wexler's life. The story *Milk and Oranges*, from which the title of this book is derived, appears in this section. What would life be without our animal pals? Stories about four-footed friends and loved ones in **Animal Magnetism**. **The Passing Parade** features fiction and prose observations on the changes in our fast-paced world.

Milk and Oranges, is a collection of short fiction—examining life, love, and the tragedy and comedy of the human condition.

**For more information
visit: SpeakingVolumes.us**

Now Available!
CHARLENE WEXLER'S

Farewell to South Shore series
Laughter and Tears series

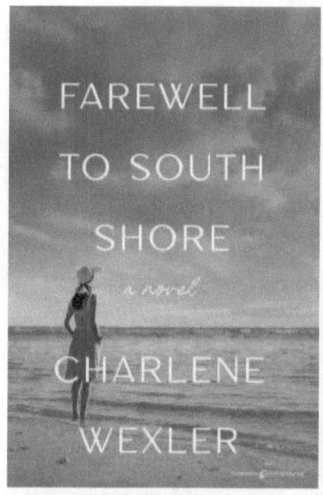

**For more information
visit: SpeakingVolumes.us**

New Release!

ANNE SHAW HEINRICH

The Women of Paradise County series
Book One – Book Two

For more information
visit: SpeakingVolumes.us

www.ingramcontent.com/pod-product-compliance
Lightning Source LLC
LaVergne TN
LVHW091633070526
838199LV00044B/1045